THE DREAMING

ANDRE BAGOO

THE DREAMING

PEEPAL TREE

First published in Great Britain in 2022
Peepal Tree Press Ltd
17 King's Avenue
Leeds LS6 1QS
England

ISBN13: 9781845235369

Printed in the United Kingdom
by Severn, Gloucester,
on responsibly sourced paper

MIX
Paper from
responsible sources
FSC
www.fsc.org
FSC® C022174

Supported using public funding by
ARTS COUNCIL
ENGLAND

CONTENTS

These are but dreaming men. Breathe, and they fade.

— Dylan Thomas, 'I Fellowed Sleep'

HAIRCUTS

1.

I found another place to get my hair cut when I moved to Woodbrook. Wally, it was rumoured, had cut the hair of the former prime minister and at least three government ministers. He wore all black. He didn't speak much. He held my head like an unusual specimen. He asked what I did, which newspaper I wrote for. He didn't ask what I wanted done. He sized me up then started to comb and cut, all the while engaging in crosstalk with some of the other hairdressers in the salon, which was filled with gurgling fountains and Laughing Buddhas.

It was a bad haircut. My side part was crooked, lengths were mismatched, and the gentle down that had accumulated on my neck was left intact, so I had to borrow Stephan's razor and shave it off myself in the shower the next day. I found this half-finished job odd. Wally was a household name. He had been in Woodbrook for decades, had branched out and now had several salons on both islands. His fees were not exorbitant, but they certainly weren't low. I chalked it up to me being a new customer or Wally having an off day. Stephan was a regular. It was near to where we lived so I went back.

The second time, I told Wally I just wanted everything neatened and trimmed; he interpreted this as a desire for something bouffant and mushroom-like. The 80s was back in style. When I got home that afternoon, Stephan said Wally should have asked before giving me "a Patrick Swayze". I chalked it up to me being unclear in my instructions. Maybe he had an off day. Stephan was a regular. It was near to where we lived. I went back.

The third time, I bumped into a high-profile lawyer who looked surprised to see me there. She had only a few weeks ago been involved in a scandal of sorts, quitting her post on a cabinet-appointed commission of inquiry. I had interviewed her. She smiled and said how good it was to see me again as she left, her hair perfectly blown out. Wally asked me how I knew her, as I showed him a photograph of what I wanted to have done with my hair. He remarked that people with my kind of hair would not be able to achieve that effect, but he would do something similar.

The result looked nothing like the image I'd saved on my phone. I couldn't say what went wrong – that was the worst part. It had a passive-aggressive quality in how underwhelming it was, this haircut, as though the barest minimum had been done so as not to be a zog, but also not enough done to be a decent haircut. In those days, I was loathe to accept that sometimes people gave you bad service not because they can't do better but because they'd rather you didn't come back. I came to accept that most of the people in Wally's salon didn't want a journalist around. Neither did he.

I had the opposite problem in my previous place. Indira's salon was right next to the newspaper. All of us in the paper's three-man politics department went there regularly. In most barbershops and salons, people discuss the news. In this one, they broke out in soliloquies. I'd be forced to listen – held down in the chair by Indira's heavy nylon bib – as customers and other people passing through loudly engaged in debate about the budget or the latest resignation or the latest on crime which, as always, was spiralling. On the one hand, I relished hearing all these perspectives. It was a good chance to get a feel for what people were saying "on the ground". On the other hand, these outbursts had a staged air. I felt goaded. I just wanted somewhere I could relax for half hour as someone washed my hair with warm water and gently fingered my scalp with fragrant oils.

Once, fed up with the old lady who would come into the salon to berate Jack Warner and Keith Rowley every time I happened to be there, I tried another place in the mall down the street. The mall was called Excellent City Centre. There was nothing excellent about it. There was a big department store with a perpetually shifting layout; a small bakery that sold greasy pastries, dry sandwiches, mahi mahi wraps, and frosted cakes; on the upper level there were kiosks selling electronics, clothes and stationery. There was a food court where I'd go sometimes to buy steamed cassava, broccoli and stir-fried chicken. On this floor, one of the clothing stores was, in fact, also a salon. There were two barbers inside and the owner, Paula, did nails.

The first time at Paula's, Francisco cut my hair. Handsome and chatty, he talked to me about his weekend, an epic party on the beach at Salybia. He recommended I try puncheon because I'd said I'd never tried it when he asked. His haircut was quick and sharp, like his conversation: the fade on the sides perfect, and he didn't charge much – about the price of lunch. He smiled and told me to come back soon.

The next time I went back, Franciso had vanished. Paula, whose plastic crucifix at her nail station made plain that she was deeply religious, declared he no longer worked there but Marco, the other barber, would be happy to cut my hair. Marco looked at me as though I was a chore, then, after a few tentative starts, took about two hours to cut my short tresses. The end result looked bizarre. He'd shaved off my widow's peak but the hairline was crooked. My forehead looked large and I seemed perpetually to be turning to the left.

I went back to Indira armed with earbuds. I felt bad at first, because this could be interpreted as rude. But I never actually played anything, I kept the music off so I could talk to Indira if she felt like chatting with me. One day, as she cut my hair (no complaints), I noticed she was breathing heavily and asked if she was okay. She said she was having health problems. The salon closed a few months later, leaving the old lady with no place to vent her frustration about the Ministry of Works and Transport.

2.

Saturdays was when Mother would give me a trim. She'd set up a stool or a chair in the kitchen of our home in Belmont, bring out a flat comb and her sharpest scissors. I wasn't sure where she had learned to cut hair, or if she had learned anywhere at all. But she never showed any hesitation. Her grasp was firm and deliberate as she cupped my head, held my hair up as though lifting the bonnet of a car. Sometimes, because she had to angle the comb and the clippers a certain way, her fingers brushed against my scalp and this hurt because of her rings. I always hated those rings. They seemed warnings about the hard transactions of the world. But I loved these Saturdays.

One year, in secondary school, around the time I fell in love with the new boy from Fatima College, I asked Mother to shave my head bald. She used Father's shaver (this was before Father left us). He asked why I wanted to go bald, and I said I just wanted to go back to my roots. In truth, I wanted to disappear, to be somebody else. When I went to class that week, I removed my glasses. The guy I had a crush on said hello, shook my hand and introduced himself to me as though I were a new student. I told him who I really was, and he laughed and said how I looked completely different. For a moment, he kept his hand in my hand. It felt like a soft bird. Then he pulled away.

Eventually, I got my hair cut by the barber on Jerningham Avenue. Johnnie had recently moved from the Circular Road. He said he moved for the bigger space, but there had been a shooting near the space on the Circular Road. I thought he'd moved because that part of Belmont was too rough. In those days, there was a local designer on Jerningham Avenue, some jewellers and some shops selling crafts. The Trinidad Theatre Workshop had bought the pretty gingerbread house on the corner, though it was way too small to be a real theatre space. Johnnie was not far from all of this and he seemed to have more clients than ever when I started going there.

Johnnie's haircuts were good. Once, I told him I felt for a change. Maybe something like Darren Ganga's hair? He looked at me as though he realised something about me for the first time.

The next time I got a haircut, Johnnie was halfway through when he started to ask me about my skin. That week, I'd started to break out again but it wasn't anything out of the ordinary. It's just your run-of-the-mill spot, I said. No, he said, it wasn't, it's a boil. I laughed at what seemed a huge exaggeration: you could barely see the thing. But he wasn't laughing when he told me not to come back to his barbershop.

3.

Cummings Kalipersad comes here you know, she said, and Verne Ramesar.

This was Claire, of Hair by Claire, who insisted on name-dropping. A friend had recommended her. She had a small salon in Maraval, not far from Burger King and SuperPharm but you'd swear it was in Beverly Hills. When she found out I was a reporter she started regaling me with the big name broadcasters on the island who were regulars (though I never saw any of them when I went). One time, after a particularly stressful month in which I'd been banned from covering parliament by the government, she had a class of trainee hairdressers. As she combed and cut my hair, she called them over to observe.

The first time I'd walked into Hair by Claire, Claire said she could tell just from my face I was fed up. I needed something new. Thereafter followed a series of bold, rather ill-advised, experiments. First came the highlights and perm, which made me look slightly like Tina Turner. Then, the low sides with the cut eyebrows, which gave me the air of a cartel leader. I'd started to go grey (Claire insisted it was premature, but I knew it ran in the family) so dyeing was a must. Blond, blue then a beautiful shade of rose. The novelty felt oppressive: I wanted to go back to where things had been. I asked her to just dye my hair black. Claire called over her students and told them to observe my scalp, as though there was some defect in it they should take note of. I felt like a freak and started to sweat under the attention.

4.

One day, Stephan came home from Wally's. He had continued to go there even though I no longer did. Wally, apparently, had never noticed that I was gone; at least he didn't ask Stephan about my absence. It was as though in his eyes we weren't a couple.

Stephan was upset, which was unusual for him. I often compared him to the potted cacti he collected: prickly but cool. He had asked Wally to cut his hair a certain way and Wally didn't. It was the third time in a row, apparently, something like this had happened. So Stephan resolved never to go back.

My friend Finn recommended a place in West Mall called Farina's. There was no appointment system, you just walked in, took a chit, waited a little and then walked into a chair. There were five hairdressers, but the first time I went I got Farina herself. I had not long quit my job, and she was decidedly unimpressed when I said I was a "freelance writer". So, halfway through the conversation I added I was also a "published author" and her eyes lit up. She had recently returned from America and had many, many ideas about how the country could be improved.

Farina was on to her ideas for how the highway interchange could be redesigned when she asked me why my hair was so dusty. It wasn't dusty as far as I could tell, just a little grey but that was nothing she hadn't seen before. She didn't pick up on my joke. Then she asked when last I'd washed my hair and I thought this was to get me to have it washed, but I'd washed my hair that very day. When I told her this, she said I was lying. My hair smelled, she said, and I should wash my hair and wash it properly because dusty hair was a hazard to her as she was sensitive to dust.

I told Stephan about this and he expressed surprise because he said she had been so nice to him when she cut his hair right after cutting mine. I wondered if I was being Wallied again. What was it about me that was so different from Stephan? He was fairer, yes, came from a prominent and well-known family – but those things didn't matter anymore. Child marriage had been abolished, we'd had a woman prime minister, for crying out loud.

The next time we went to Farina's, the girl at the front asked if I preferred any specific barber to cut my hair. I said anyone but Farina. Someone suppressed a laugh and it was then that I decided I would return to Farina's as often as possible, just to annoy her.

5.

Things were tight after I broke up with Stephan, so I found a new place on Queen Street. Like most streets downtown, it was home to street-dwellers who slept on cardboard boxes and kept their things in supermarket carts. There were a few jewellery and furniture stores, and an empty mall in which Jeremiah cut hair on the third floor.

Jeremiah had a child and always talked about her. What subjects she was studying (geography was her favourite). How many books she read. The wise and clever remarks she made. The glowing report cards she brought home. He also talked about her good-for-nothing mother who, I was to understand, was unreliable, toxic, irresponsible, but nonetheless had custody of his child.

It was only after some time that I realised Jeremiah wasn't just talkative, he was always drunk. I realised this when, one day, with half my hair cut and the other half wild and unbridled, he asked me if I'd like a drink. He was going to take a break and grab a beer from the bar around the corner on Frederick Street. A few minutes later, he returned with the beer, placed it on his counter, and carried on as normal, talking about Sheba and all the wickedness she was up to with little Geraldine.

The next time it happened, Jeremiah didn't come back until half hour later. But I'd developed a rapport with him. I liked his haircuts and they were cheap. I just told him I was in a rush and it would be better not to have too many breaks next time.

The last time I saw him, he nicked my ears with his razor, the cut burned when he sprayed me with alcohol. I was still bleeding when I got home.

6.

I went back to living with Stephan, even though we had broken up, because I couldn't afford a place on my own now that I didn't have a regular salary. I paid half the rent and we were still friends so it was fine.

I repurposed the office into a bedroom, used pallets to make a bed (I'd seen this on YouTube). I started to paint a lot because my therapist said it might help and some people actually bought a few paintings. A guy down south even started to print T-shirts with my paintings on them, which I wore to parties as a way of promoting myself.

One day, our landlord said she was raising the rent. She also said a new guy was moving into the apartment next to ours.

Angelo, it turned out, was a hairdresser. His family was originally from Venezuela but had been living in the country for generations. He had a heavy Spanish accent, and people often took him for one of the migrants you'd see in the news fleeing Maduro. He worked at a salon around the corner.

Angelo was clearly popular with men. There were all the burly guys who helped him move his stuff in. Then, the men who came to several house-warmings (his place was small so he had multiple events). During the week, our courtyard was quiet as I wrote late into the night. But early in the mornings I would hear Angelo's door open and then someone would slink through the gate.

A month after Angelo moved in, he started to blast gospel

music in the mornings. I thought this odd. But when I started to get to know him, I realised Angelo was genuinely religious. And he had a side-hustle. He was praying, not having sex, with all of the men who came to see him. Apparently, they were all seeking a way not to be gay anymore. I found this out the hard way when, after he had agreed to give me a trim in his small living room, he started asking me about my problems and then proceeded to tell me about His Saviour Jesus Christ. He prayed for me, carefully holding his blade, as he gave me a mark.

7.

The Christmas Stephan moved out, he left me a parting gift. I expected it to be another cactus or maybe another set of journals or stationery. When I opened it, it was a really nice shaver, an expensive one. He said I could use it to cut my own hair. For a moment, a pang of regret came over me. Things hadn't worked out with Stephan (he was moving in with his new boyfriend) and I was going to miss him. I was going to miss, too, how the apartment was filled with all kinds of cacti – bunny ears, pear, chollas, the showy schlumbergera with its fuchsia flowers.

I tried to get a new roommate. It was a tough sell. The landlord had raised the rent again, and the economy was in the toilet so there were few takers. I asked a few ex's if they were interested and they politely declined. Two friends of friends came to look at the space, but they didn't seem impressed. I'd forgotten how, sometimes, when lovers move into a space, that space is perfect no matter what. When the love fades, suddenly you see all the flaws.

After a few months of paying the rent on my own, I could go on no longer.

On my last day in the apartment, I sat in the empty kitchen and searched haircut videos on the internet. It was pretty easy, I realised, once you had the guard rails for the shaver. The problem was, of course, the back. And the fancier things like marks. But with guards you could wing it. And who needed marks, really? I took out the really nice shaver and plugged it into a socket. Small lights at the side glimmered; it glowed alive like a spaceship. I put the length setting of the guard on seven, turned it on, and combed it through my hair. Nothing happened. I set it to three, for a shorter length, and tried again. Sure enough, hair began to drop to the sink, to my feet, to the floor, silver and dark flakes softly falling like the years had passed me by. If the result was a little uneven, a little jagged near the temples, I didn't care. With practice I would get better.

At least Mom wouldn't have to cut my hair.

CONUNDRUM

If he were honest, the leg was okay but not wow. There it was, a stubby, artless thing, impressively muscular yet impassive, drowned in the hazy sea of the sepia filter. Newton clicked 'like', not because of any particular enthusiasm but because he felt this was the kind of thing he had to do. He had to put himself out there, ensure he was seen, let it be known that he liked legs and well-toned legs too.

The leg belonged to Duane, a trainer Newton followed on Instagram. Duane had a boyfriend but was into books and, on learning Newton was a poet, followed Newton back and expressed an interest in Newton's writing. This was the previous July; then the interest petered out, as it inevitably did when people read Newton's work, but both men continued to like each other's posts every now and then in the awkward netherworld between indifference and not wanting to offend by unfollowing.

Newton had recently deleted Grindr again. Men there were weird, flaky or not interesting. Whenever he thought he'd found someone who might want to do more than exchange dick pics, he would send a face pic and they would fall silent. He didn't understand this. He wasn't that old and, in the right lighting, he was rather attractive with his cute dimples, his manly Roman nose (his father's), intense eyes and long eyelashes (his mother's). His fashion sense was nothing to write home about, consisting of smart glasses, plaid shirts, and multiple pairs of converse sneakers – but didn't that qualify as "geek chic" these days? He was marketable, a catch, in fact. And weren't people attracted to poets? Hadn't that worked for Byron, Shelley, Keats, Rimbaud? Talent, creativity, passion, a profound engagement with the world – what man on Grindr could resist?

It wasn't just the men online. It was the cool, pretty boys at Boycode parties, the Muscle Marys at Carnival fetes, the slightly pretentious gays at Drink! Wine Bar, the drunk, sketchy gays at Club Studio, the nerds at his NALIS book club and the artsy, sexually fluid crowd at galleries and backyard art spaces – all of whom rebuffed his wines and attempts at small talk.

While gay Trinidad was reluctant to embrace him, straight Trinidad couldn't get enough of him. Newton was caught up in dalliances with ostensibly heterosexual men, all of whom he felt were slightly crazy or at least confused. He knew enough about closet cases to impose clear limits. He lowered his expectations again and again and told himself it was just sex, not love. Yet still, some of these men lingered in his mind, hard rocks in his sea of longings. If only one – just one – could find the courage to be truthful, to love him and to love him openly. If only.

It was in a half-depressed, half-bored mood that he scrolled through the list of people who had liked Duane's leg-day post, an action he didn't find the least stalkerish. It was research. Most of the men who approved of the leg were probably gay or, at the very least, interested in the male body. He followed anyone on the list whose profile was pleasant. Put yourself out there, he thought.

Klaus followed back immediately. Newton had never seen his profile, recognized none of his friends, and could not be sure what country he was in, though he thought Klaus had that charming, sharp look that indicated he was definitely a Trini. Klaus had a handsome face with a big, hipster beard and a

Bollywood vibe. He was evidently obsessed with working out. Every post was from the gym. One with his biceps flexed. A video of him doing pull-ups (a cocky bulge visible in his joggers). An image of him throwing a tyre around. It was the kind of thing Newton was attracted to but normally passed over because he thought such men were compensating for some emotional or physical deficiency or were in the throes of some kind of body dysmorphia against which he'd never be able to compete. Today, though, he didn't have much to lose.

In the first few minutes of their interaction, Klaus liked thirty of Newton's Instagram posts, a gesture that Newton found more ambiguous than it was. Was it a clear red flag: too eager too soon? Or just a safe way of expressing interest without explicitly doing so? It could have been a routine series of likes, the way some young people swipe and swipe and swipe, all the while clicking 'like' without much real deliberation. There was only one way to find out.

Over the course of the day, they spoke about their shared love of rainy nights, the pros and cons of vegan diets, body sculpting (Klaus commented on images of Newton at the beach; Newton asked about Klaus' pull-up technique), life-changing moments in their childhoods, favourite places to go. These exchanges felt amiable but not quite flirtatious. Still, Newton was pleased with any attention he could get. Then, around the middle of the afternoon (it was a slow day for Klaus, who worked in a big pharmacy on Wrightson Road) Klaus asked him about his poetry.

It is a truth universally acknowledged that obscure, mid-career poets like nothing more than a chance to talk about their work. The question was like a shot of heroin. Newton spoke of the origins of all five of his books, the painstaking process of finalising each manuscript, his experiences with various publishers and the literary elite of the island, his models and

influences, the pitfalls of trying to market poetry in an environment inclined to prose, and his plans for future books. Maybe,
he said, a selected is due, because he was advancing in age
though in truth 34 wasn't really that old, as 29-year-old Klaus
pointed out.

Then Klaus told Newton he had a secret he wanted to share.
He, too, was a poet. Could he email Newton the manuscript
for a book he was going to publish?

A sinkhole opened in Newton's stomach. Of course, he
said, even as he weighed the likelihood that the whole interaction with Klaus had been meant to serve this one purpose
alone. Such things had happened to Newton before. The thrill
of somebody new would give way to a manuscript being
sprung on him at the earliest opportunity. It was flattering. His
judgment was valued. But even this he could not be sure of. He
got little sense any of these closet writers had ever read his
work.

Klaus's book was 150 pages, a fact that Newton noted with
apprehension, since poetry books these days were half that
length. He opened the book. Each poem was short; they
consisted of lyrics like:

> if you are the cliff
> i am the mountain
> we are one and yet not one
>
> savour this moment
> before we both fall
> to the sky
>
> — *K.*

and

patience is
sand
falling through
an hourglass
is knowing when
to turn over
a new leaf
confident
the bottle
will never run out

— *K.*

and

we are broken
my heart
yearns for you
but I know my heart
and I know it enough
to know what I cannot
know
your body
our story
the stars, their faults!
all our crimes
opening
like a hibiscus
the river flows
to the sea
of forgiveness

— *K.*

The poems were not bad. But they were not exactly good either. Actually, maybe they were bad. Perhaps with a little editing, a little shaping, they could become less like something you might have once read on Tumblr, a little less wannabe Rupi Kaur and more Klaus Antoine. Perhaps they could, over time, work together to excavate Klaus' voice? Despite his misgivings, later that night, Newton found himself, after he'd sat down and read the book from cover to cover, conveying praise for Klaus' poetry. He focused only on the positive and professed love for what he had read and even asked to see more. In response, Klaus suggested they do a book swap. Maybe they could meet somewhere and exchange titles. Klaus had published three books with a local vanity press and had extra copies.

The next book was longer. Klaus said he was interested in the epic, not as a form but as a mode of living. It was called *You Are the Star of Your Own Movie* and was divided into 12 sections, each named after a famous film. As they sat close to each other on the sofa of the Rituals coffee house on Maraval Road, Newton complimented Klaus on the cover – a photograph of a vintage television set. Privately, he thought that was probably the best part of the book. Newton was promising to read the volume later at home when he felt Klaus put a warm, clammy hand on his. Newton reciprocated by holding Klaus's hand, discretely, as they sat sipping vanilla lattes and talking about puppies and inventing stories for all the people who walked past the large window outside.

That night, Newton read the opening poem and cringed. Then the dilemma he now faced dawned on him. He couldn't encourage this poetry thing too much. He had limited time in between all the freelance magazine articles he had to write on pompous business executives, up-and-coming soca stars, and "entrepreneurs" selling various varieties of soaps. He wanted to be able to devote more time to his own writing. Despite his small-town, local renown, it remained a fact that he was a minor poet in the larger scheme of things. While his current destitution might one day yield to success, while he might possibly break through and become a household name – the author of unprecedented Caribbean poetry bestsellers – that could not happen unless he had enough time to work on follow-ups to his own books, all of which were inspired by the poetry of the obscure English poet Heathcote Williams and contained moving dedications to his favourite Caribbean authors: Derek Walcott, Martin Carter, Lorna Goodison, and Dionne Brand.

More worryingly, though Klaus said he was open to constructive criticism, Newton knew enough from his own experience that any criticism at all might dampen things between them. Criticism, no matter how couched, always left a crater from the impact – another universal truth poets know. It doesn't matter how softly the meteor lands. He texted Klaus. I LOVE your book! Come over for dinner tomorrow and we can talk more about it.

★

They had been boyfriends six months when Klaus sprung the surprise on Newton. He turned up outside Newton's apartment in Tunapuna, grinning wildly as he told Newton to get dressed (semi-casual was fine). For all the control he liked to exercise over his life, Newton loved Klaus's surprises. He enjoyed them the way only a control freak enjoys being able, at last, to cede power. This was equally the case in the bedroom, where Klaus, with his obscene torso, was strangely warm and affectionate, even as his lovemaking was merciless. His insatiability, too, drove Newton mad – the way the idea of someone desiring you so much was almost as pleasurable as the sex itself. And when he cried out Klaus' name during sex (this was the only unsatisfactory part of their sex life, who in Trinidad named their son Klaus?) he did so with a joy and a relish he had never experienced before.

They drove to Pasea Village, then turned into Prescott Lane and parked outside a building with a sign that said Inkaholix Tattoo Studio. Klaus had arranged for them to get identical tattoos: an acrostic poem written by him that spelled out *Newton*. Newton paused, but only for the slightest moment, for he had long crossed the line when to criticise any aspect of Klaus's poetry would betray a deception. And what did it matter that the tepid verse would forever be etched into his flesh? He put the matter of quality out of his mind and focused on what lay behind the gesture. He told Klaus how moved he was, how wonderful this was, and they made love again that night with their bandages on. Newton didn't know this but as he slept, Klaus watched him carefully, love in his knowing eyes.

The day they moved in together, Klaus walked with rolls of newspaper print. He unrolled them, used stencils to paint poems on them and hung them up at various parts of the new apartment. This they had gotten at a good rate, though it was a little far away in Arima. Newton got some potted palms, which he placed so as to ensure that most of the posters would be obscured once the plants had grown tall enough. The space began to look like one of those chic beige and green millennial apartments he had seen on Instagram.

Months later, Klaus asked Newton if he would show one of his manuscripts to Newton's publisher. Newton had, as the years went by, continued to plod away at his writing. He had reached the stage where he would be asked to moderate panels at the local literary festival, or sometimes read his poems at an art gallery or two. Once, the University of the West Indies even asked him to participate in a colloquium on the Pierrot Grenade after his poem on that Carnival character had been published in *Callaloo*. The event had been a success. Fifteen people came and Newton was heartened by the largest audience he had yet drawn. He wondered for a moment if he should show his publisher his boyfriend's work. Would he not embarrass himself with the most important contact he had in the publishing world? Then he thought of something else: if he did send the book to Chicken Barrow Press and they rejected it, this would actually let *them* tell Klaus what Newton never could.

In these times of relative happiness in Arima, he would think of the old days when he would have desperate sex with guys who insisted they were straight; who would refuse to kiss him even as they drilled deeper and deeper into him like oil derricks in search of the truth, a truth that they would find only when they came, momentarily holding his hand, clasping love, then letting go, getting up and wiping themselves off before driving away into the night.

No, what he had with Klaus was not one of these mangled torments of stepping forward while stepping backwards, of private desire and public denial. No, it was not confused. It was full of real promise, it was full of real joy, even in imperfection, and Newton would do nothing, nothing to ever dampen that. And if that meant pretending to love somebody's poetry more than he really did, that white lie was a small price he was happy to pay. So he delegated. He sent off Klaus' manuscript (*Crossfires of Hurricanes*) with a little prefatory note and waited. But instead of getting the definitive rejection email he had hoped for, there was no response from Chicken Barrow Press, a silence that in itself was a response. He said as much to Klaus months later. But Klaus, instead of considering this some kind of signal about his work, saw Chicken Barrow's silence as a form of disrespect against Newton, who was undoubtedly one of their best authors.

★

It was two months after they adopted the rescue dog that the request came in. The programming director of a literary festival in Montserrat wrote to Klaus asking him to read his poetry at that year's edition of their festival. The director had seen Klaus' website, which Klaus had heavily invested in, getting graphic designers to refine it over the years. They were interested in featuring Klaus on a panel on poets and social media. Newton was terrified of the idea of Klaus reading his poems publicly. He wasn't jealous. He had never heard of – what was the name of the festival? – he looked again at the email Klaus was showing him. It was from the Alliouagana Festival of the Word. He had never heard of the Alliouagana Festival but the thought of Klaus reading his poetry aloud anywhere, at any time, in front of any crowd was too much to bear. What if they snickered? What if they laughed?

Before one thought had been completed, another one dawned. Perhaps he was wrong. Perhaps he was missing something. Klaus had been invited after all. Poetry is a subjective thing. And many people might genuinely enjoy Klaus' work. (But it was good Montserrat was small and difficult to reach from Trinidad: not many people Newton knew would be there.) How had things gotten this far? A molehill had, over the years, become a mountain, all snaking back to that Monday when Klaus had first emailed him his PDF and Newton had responded positively, knowing, from his own experience, just how alluring the idea of someone approving your work is, knowing how poets, even the cool and aloof ones, secretly crave approval, secretly want confirmation that they have been seen.

Newton now felt deeply ashamed whenever the issue arose. Mercifully, these instances were, thanks to their newfound domestic bliss, increasingly rare because they did so many other things with each other. Even before Beatrice had come into their lives they had glided along a never-ending stream of dinner dates, road trips to Toco and Mayaro, parties at the houses of friends, vacations in Tobago, and fetes at secret and exciting locations revealed at the last minute by the organisers. Now, they were devoting all their time to buying Beatrice treats, buying Beatrice cute outfits, setting Beatrice up on play dates and organising appointments for Beatrice to go to the vet, to go to the groomer, even assembling new storage units to keep Beatrice's things in their apartment, which was getting too small for the three of them. So, Newton worried about the Alliouagana Festival for only a few days, then decided it would be a nice vacation and began to look forward to the trip. But then, a particularly active hurricane season caused the cancellation of that year's festival, much to Klaus' disappointment.

★

It was when they got engaged that Newton could bear it no longer. He thought of telling Klaus in a poem, which he even drafted on his laptop while Klaus slept next to him in bed, smelling of that cologne with notes of bergamot and coconut that he always wore. He even gave the poem a grand title but then decided against it. He was not going to hide behind a poem. He was going to tell Klaus in person. Two months after getting engaged, however, he had cause to see his therapist. He needed to thrash things out further. The night before the appointment he pulled up the draft of the poem, deleted it, then pulled it back out of the trash.

Newton had not seen Ms Gardenia in a while. She had given him all the tools he needed since his breakdown many years before when his parents threw him out. The long stretches in which he managed not to see her were both cost-effective and a sign of his progress as a human being. There's nothing wrong with considering the feelings of others, Ms Gardenia said, sitting in her cosy, book-lined office in Woodbrook. Yes, she said, yes you may have censored yourself in the past but I doubt that will be a deal-breaker in this relationship. Perhaps you should consider whether your anxiety about this issue is coming from somewhere else.

After a few days of reflecting, Newton could think of nothing that might be on his mind. They were engaged and that was that. He had no doubt Klaus was the love of his life. They were different, but somehow just fitted together in a way no analysis could explain. There was a chemistry and a spark which, after so many years, remained undimmed. They could not get married in Trinidad, so they decided to fly to Puerto Rico to marry, honeymoon in Old San Juan, then return to Trinidad where they would have a private commitment ceremony in Tobago.

Was he anxious? He asked the question aloud one day when he was home alone, petting Beatrice, who was trying to get him to play with the brand new stuffed donkey they had given her. Maybe it was just nerves. Then he made a resolution. He would tell him after the wedding. The first one, that is.

But the first wedding came and went (for some reason, Klaus stuck to prose when he made his vows) and they were preoccupied with having a good time in Old San Juan, visiting the old fort that looked like a giant morocoy, and clubbing in the big rococo lounges in the city, with their plush red curtains and their truckloads of well-groomed, metrosexual men and painted women. When, the commitment ceremony happened in Tobago, Newton actually forgot his promise, and the sun set magnificently on their ceremony on the beach.

★

Three weeks after their fifth anniversary, Newton woke to find he was alone. The house was quiet. The workmen renovating the kitchen were not due to arrive until ten. But he could hear shuffling downstairs. It was probably Klaus in the living room doing yoga. Klaus was always up so bloody early. Newton shuffled to the bathroom, washed his face and looked at himself in the mirror. So this is what forty-six looks like, he thought, his salt and pepper hair ruffled, his body not exactly ripped, but still rather comely all things considered. There it was on his right ribcage:

> now &
> ever
> we'll be
> together
> only diamonds &
> nights
>
> — K.

Perhaps it was even reassuring that while his body had changed, the text remained, a relic of what seemed a different dimension of time altogether. He chuckled.

Newton and Klaus had both stopped writing for a while now. Life had a way of sorting things out and showing them new priorities. Those priorities inevitably revolved around their love for each other, their child, Lamming, and the shift that happened when they both stopped dreaming of agents, book contracts, literary prizes, residencies and fellowships, when they stopped hoping for things that one day might happen and simply began to appreciate what they already had.

As he served Klaus scrambled egg whites for breakfast, Newton said, You remember those poems you used to write? The ones you were always so proud of? Klaus looked up from his coffee, intently, patiently. God, he was still so handsome, Newton thought, before continuing. You know I never really liked them that much. Newton sliced some bread, but paused, ever so slightly. Klaus shovelled some avocado and egg whites into his mouth and got up. Of course you didn't, he said, you loved me so much you pretended to. When you got that tattoo with me, I knew. You would do anything for me. And then he wolfed down the rest of his breakfast on his feet because the workmen were coming and Lamming would soon be awake.

SIMPLE THINGS

New signs had been put up and right above him was one
saying:

VISION STATEMENT

Eric Williams Medical Sciences Complex
Neonatal Intensive Care Unit

To provide quality, technological, professional
services to all clients requiring expert, continuous
specialised care.
Our highly skilled professional staff who can
make quick, accurate and life-saving decisions that
would ensure all clients receive competent care.

Something about the sign riled him. Maybe it was the way it
referred to babies as clients, as though they bounce out of the
womb wearing jackets and ties, holding folders and pens, ready
to issue instructions to their custodians. Was it even English?
The part about accurate decisions made him bristle too, imply-
ing there was always one right answer, always an easy, clear-cut
path for treatment. Not the messy complications of medicine
shortages, malfunctioning equipment, nursing incompetence
– in addition to the cases when a doctor has to consider pain,
evaluate questions about long-term quality of life, and untan-

gle the messy ethical conflicts caused by parents wanting to foist their religious beliefs on babies who have not yet had the chance to contemplate the Mysteries of Life, such as whether God exists or not. But he quickly stowed these thoughts away, as he had been trained to do, and considered the task at hand.

Focus.

To save this baby's life, he would first have to put it in a bag. Its lungs were not working properly. Its chest was a small balloon expanding and contracting, expanding and contracting – but with difficulty. Soft ribs and cartilage moved beneath paper-thin skin. For most babies, breathing comes naturally. For this one, breathing was a Herculean effort. If he did not act fast, in a few minutes its muscles would get sore and seize up, and its own body would become an iron cage squeezing it to death. Respiratory failure. He prepared the cushion-rimmed face-mask. He prepared the oxygen. He gently encased the child's body with the pouch, the way you might put a small turkey into a baking bag to seal vital fluids. After a few minutes of pumping air, the baby was ready for the next life-saving procedure: intubation.

Focus.

This is what he knew: in the world of caring for sick babies, the difference between tragedy and triumph is measured in the smallest of units: grams, minutes. A baby less than 600 grams was normally a lost cause. Even if you could get such a baby to live, it would be damaged for life. That's what they never tell you in movies and on TV. A baby born after less than 26 weeks in the womb has an 80 per cent chance of dying. If it lives, it has a hundred per cent chance of having a terrible birth defect. Hundred per cent. A virtual certainty.

This baby was 23 weeks, 409 grams. Too young, too small when they sent it down to him from the ward upstairs. What was he supposed to do? Tell the orderlies to turn around and take it straight to the morgue? He gathered the equipment he needed. Laryngoscope with straight blades, extra bulbs and batteries (in case there was another outage), endotracheal tubes, a stylet, scissors, tape for securing the device to the tube (this was crucial), alcohol sponges, a capnograph to measure CO_2 levels.

In another country, high-risk births like this one would have been detected long ago, those likely to need resuscitation anticipated, additional skilled personnel would be on hand, necessary equipment gathered and medication administered in advance. But this was Trinidad.

He needed to see the vocal cords. Putting the tube in the wrong place could mean the difference between the baby becoming an opera singer or a mute. He put in the laryngo-scope in order to see the cords. At first the epiglottis, the curtain of flesh at the back of the throat, did not open, but it soon gave way. He moved to put the tube in. The room was cold. But beneath his scrubs it was the Sahara. He could feel a bead of sweat form near his temples, cool and seep back into his hair. Slowly, slowly. Then success: the tube was in place. He taped it down so it could not shift. He'd reached the stage when there was only one thing he could do.

Wait.

This was another thing you don't see on Netflix. The helplessness after every possible option has been exhausted, every step taken, every appropriate course of action judiciously measured and implemented. He looked at the being in front of him. The miracle. Somebody's dream. Somebody's labour of love. Not even the size of two fists put together. A little jewel box ready to be filled with riches. Eye-protection pads too large, obscuring most of its face. Dolly arms and legs akimbo amid the tape and tubes and wires. A soft, dusky-red thing so still and mesmerising you wondered if time had stopped, if all the oxygen had left the room, and you were suspended in limbo along with it. He reread the card at the side of the incubator. The parents had named the baby.

Charlie.

Stay alive for me Charlie, he said. The towering machine that warmed the baby's body beeped. And beeped.

Wait.

Wait.

Wait.

He saw the dog on the way to his date with Usha. It must have been one of the dogs from the park. It was at the side of the road, sniffing a pile of rubbish. Like any other you might see in Woodbrook: a young dog, a black and white mongrel, between a husky and a pariah, very like a fox in the face, running up and down the pavement looking uneasily from side to side, wondering where its next meal would come from.

Usha wanted to meet for dinner. Something was up. They'd been together for years now and never had cause to set dates. Especially just for dinner. Normally they did dinner and a movie. Dinner on the way to a fete. Dinner on the way to board games in Chaguanas (she tolerated his geeky passion for Wizard's Academy). No, dinner for dinner's sake signalled something that could not take place in their apartment.

It was a slow night at The Veranda, a restaurant in an old gingerbread house on a drowsy side-street of the city. At another time, the emptiness would have kindled a warm, cosy feeling. Today, the house, with its white latticework, seemed ghostly. Usha cleared her throat, uncomfortably.

How was your shift? she asked, moving her wineglass closer to herself as if to hide behind it.

As soon as she asked the question, he saw baby Charlie's dead body. It was bad, but it's over, he said.

What was bad about – you know what? Never mind, she said. I'm sorry to hear it was bad. She avoided making eye contact with him, feigned interest in the cocktail menu.

How is the gallery? he asked, looking at her head wrap. She had recently taken to wearing head wraps, inspired by her favourite author, Zadie Smith. Today's was a bright red, which matched her lipstick and picked up tones from her dress. It was a simple black dress with cap sleeves and colourful stripes along the shoulders. Her hair was pulled back in a neat bun, her large rectangular glasses gave her an officious air, as though she had just come from the library.

I don't want to prolong this, she said. I want to break up.

The baked plantains he'd had for an appetiser made a cartwheel in his stomach. He quickly suppressed the impulse to vomit.

Why? he said.

I want children. I know we talked about it in Curaçao and I said I was okay with us not having any. But I just can't do it, she said.

For the first time she looked directly at him.

I know you said it has to do with your job, with all the children you see suffering. I feel it's not fair for me to give up my dream just because of your job and your fears.

I never asked you to. I just felt you understood where I was coming from, he said.

It's not fair Ravi. And I know you know that, she said. I don't think I'm asking for much.

I disagree. You're asking for a lot, he said.

A waiter came with the first course: coo coo, steamed fish, vegetables and callaloo. As always, they had ordered the same thing. The two identical meals looked like festive paintings, out of place in the funereal mood that had fallen over them. When the waiter was gone, there was an uncomfortable pause, a pregnant pause in which they both felt that what either said next might shift everything.

I used to want you to compromise on this, Usha said. But you know what I think now? Even if you did. Even if you did say, *Heck, yes let's do it*, even if you did that just for me, I can't raise children with a father who has compromised. I need someone who is wholly committed to this.

Children? he said. You said just one.

What kind of life is it if you're not leaving something behind? she said. What's the point of everything?

Maybe life's meaningless, then we die, he said.

She exhaled as though this was the kind of thing she'd grown fed up of, looked at the food on the plate, got up and said, I'll stay at Jen's tonight. You can have the apartment. I'll move out next week.

I think we should just calm down and give this –

But she was already out of the door.

He was late. It was half past nine. He'd lost track of time, drifting around the half-empty apartment. Her things were gone, and he could now see how much of the place was her. Where were all her books, with their colourful spines? Where were her records? Her paintings? Her clothes? Her station in the bathroom lay unused. He looked in the mirror and saw a defeated man. A lonely man with sad eyes and dishevelled hair. There was something childish about his features: the birthmark on his forehead that made people compare him to Harry Potter, his dark, bushy eyebrows that seemed like he was in a disguise, his small nose, his thin lips, his rounded shoulders. These days he sported a pregnant paunch that was rapidly ballooning because of his nights at the rum shop with Geronimo.

The Morbidity and Mortality Meeting was scheduled for 10 o'clock and he arrived at half past. There were stern looks. The meeting to review the case was standard procedure when a baby dies. This was another part they don't tell you about, he mused. How after having one of your patients die, you then have to face your colleagues, relive every excruciating detail, as they interrogate you over each decision, each choice. In this case, something extremely rare had happened. A small umbilical tube used as a central line to avoid repeatedly puncturing – and thereby tormenting – the baby had shifted. The slender tube had ridden up into his chest and pressure from its fluid pierced his heart. By the time there were signs of cardiac arrest, it was too late.

What do you call that? An act of God? Ravi said to Geronimo after the meeting. They were in Boscoe's Bar & Lounge, the dark, cavernous rum shop where all the stressed-out doctors went after their shift. After I did so much to save this one, for it to be undone by some simple little thing. It makes you want to give up.

What you go do? Geronimo said.

They sat listlessly in the murk, surrounded by walls plastered with faded posters. Images of buxom women and virile men. Advertisements for Mackeson, Guinness, Stag. All beverages apparently keys to becoming sex gods. Loud music boomed, but the promiscuous DJ was unable to commit to a genre: soca, dancehall – at one stage Ravi thought he heard electro. A fight broke out at a pool table to the back, but it quickly faded. A drunken patron started to dance with a dustbin as though it were a woman. Geronimo resumed the conversation.

What happen to you and Usha?

All she wants is a child and I'm not ready for that.

Wait. Wait. A woman want to have a baby with you?

Yes, Ravi said.

With you? Yuh sure?

What so hard to believe about that?

Nothing, Geronimo said. So... What's the problem with that exactly?

I didn't, well, I don't want children, Ravi said.

You don't want children, Geronimo said. Your job is to save children, but you don't want children?

I don't see any contradiction. I have a right not to want children. It's not the Dark Ages.

Of course! Geronimo said. Nothing wrong with that, nothing wrong with that at all. It's just that you seem like someone who would be a good father. What's the real reason you don't want to?

Ravi didn't know how to put into words the feeling of inadequacy he'd developed since becoming a doctor, the feeling of never being fully in control, of not being good enough, of being afraid to hold things close because you could easily lose them.

I don't know. Do I need one? Maybe I'm scared.

That's everybody! Geronimo said.

The man dancing with the dustbin began to aggressively fondle it, whispering sweet nothings.

Geronimo looked aghast, then said, Boy, you givin' up good lovin' cause yuh fraid?

Now that Geronimo had put it that way, it did seem hard to explain.

She's the love of my life but I can't give her what she wants.

Tell you what partner, Geronimo said. Get a dog.

What?

A dog, a pet. Someone to practice on, Geronimo said. Maybe then you'll discover something about yourself you never even realised.

I've killed every plant I ever had, Ravi said. How am I supposed to take care of a dog?

You just wait and see, Geronimo said. That dog will take care of you more than it own self.

Not long after Geronimo planted the idea, Ravi saw the dog again on his street. It was sniffing around the pavement. He went back inside and got the box of leftover KFC from the fridge. The gate was giving trouble again because of the wire mesh used to keep cats out. After a while he managed to fix it, get the gate open. He lured the dog into the yard with a drumstick. He let it tear into the succulent pieces of fried chicken and crunch the delectable bones. Once it was done eating, Ravi cautiously opened the door to his apartment. The dog went straight for the sofa, sitting as though it had always sat on that very spot – a new furry ornament amid the empty Carib beer cans, old newspapers, and stale, buttery popcorn kernels that had fallen between the sofa cushions.

Come boy! Ravi said.

The dog looked at him quizzically.

What should I call you?

The dog shifted its head to the right.

Mordecai?

The dog shifted its head to the left. A half-empty pack of Crix crackers dropped from the couch to the floor.

Crix?

A bark. Short, sharp.

Here Crix! Ravi said.

The dog sprung off the sofa and made its way to its new master.

He's such a fast learner, Ravi told Geronimo the next time they were at Boscoe's.

Geronimo wasn't in the mood. It was the stage of the evening when all he would do was talk about needing a good woman and being lonely and how life would have been better had he stayed with his first love, Tina, who had gone on to marry a man from the Bahamas and migrated there.

I've already taught him how to sit, to fetch, to potty outside, to go into the crate, to come out of the crate, to stay, to go, to get off the bed –

The dog sleeping on your bed? Geronimo said.

Yeah, why not?

Man, you worse than I thought.

There's research suggesting the bond between you and your dog intensifies if you share the same bed, Ravi said.

I'll tell you what will intensify – me and she in the same bed, Geronimo said. He pointed his beer in the direction of an attractive woman who reminded Ravi of Usha, a fact he was not willing to acknowledge. But despite himself, the smell of her suddenly came back to him, filled him, made him feel as though he might fall away. Her smell: cookie dough, butterscotch, cocoa butter. A rip tide tore through the centre of his body.

Crix has been having bad dreams, Ravi said. I wake up and he's crying and jerking like a possessed demon or something. I have to pat him for him to calm down.

He's remembering all the girls and them from his past life, Geronimo said. He must have been a wet man on the streets.

I don't know. I may have to call in a dog whisperer.

Or just get him neutered! Geronimo said.

The next day on the ward, Ravi was checking his mobile phone – which he used to remotely monitor the cameras he installed to make sure Crix was okay – when it happened again. The same shivering thing that happened when he had remembered Usha at Boscoe's. He shoved the feelings back into the cupboard and double padlocked it.

Don't worry Crix, I'll be home soon! he shouted into his phone, using the intercom function in the monitoring app.

Crix, who was lounging on the new armchair his master had bought for him, lifted his head to check where the strange noise was coming from, then went back to his afternoon siesta, unbothered.

Some weeks later, Ravi returned home to find Crix missing. He looked in the living room, the bedroom, the office, the mudroom where the crate was. Nothing. With alarm, he noticed one window, just above the washing machine, was unlatched – he'd forgotten to lock it. Could Crix have climbed on top the crate, then onto the machine, then out the window?

He looked in the yard. There was nothing. Then he noticed a gap in the wire mesh of the gate. That must have happened recently, he thought. Certainly, he hadn't noticed the gap that morning. Could Crix have opened it, slipped through? How could this have happened?

He wondered if Crix wanted to return to his life on the streets, a life without him. He printed the best picture he had of the dog (which was not hard because there were so many). He made a flier saying:

MISSING
Responds to "Crix"
Call 678-9291

Something feverish was rising inside him by the time he got to the park. The leaves of the trees were still, dark against the orange-purple sky. He could hear no birds. He tacked fliers onto several trees at the park's entrance. He roamed the grounds. Unusually for this time of the day, there were very few joggers. The sky went black.

He heard a strange, high-pitched vocalisation. Or was it a gust of wind? Park lampposts twinkled on. Then he heard a whine-bark, whine-bark sound and saw him in the distance, under a tree. Crix was with a dead blackbird, toying with it, using his nose to throw it from place to place like one of his rubber bones.

Naughty Crix! Leave it! Ravi said.

Its feathers were shimmering scales in the dim light. The bird's neck was broken, but the eyes sparkled as though there was still life, still something. Everything he'd been trying to process burst to the surface in one moment, like a bubble of air that swells from the depths before disappearing. The dead bird in the orange light of the lamppost. Baby Charlie's body. Usha and all she meant to him. Crix. There they all were: life and death side by side, the past and the future, the certain and the uncertain, the safe and the unsafe. It was all life. It was all okay. Something opened, something dissipated. Some idea of not being good enough, or ready enough subsided. He shivered, then realised he was crying.

When he was back home, he fixed the wire mesh on the gate and made sure Crix was safe and sound in the crate before calling Usha. The phone went straight to voicemail. He was undeterred.

If you still want to, let's reopen our discussion about children, he said into the receiver. I'm not saying this just to get you back. I'm saying this because I now realise it. I want them. And I want them with you.

He hung up the phone and started to get ready for his next shift at work.

HUNGER

Three months after the breakup, you meet Paquito. Well, at first his name isn't Paquito. It's *RightNow95*.

You'd spent the day in bed crying, listening to Taylor Swift's folklore album like it was going out of style. You'd tried everything to regain your bearings. You'd resumed counselling and signed up for yoga class at two separate studios. You'd said, yes, to every single social invitation you received until the lockdown happened. If you could still work at Wendy's, heck you'd even take an extra shift.

You're not into drugs, you don't drink, and while you're a cook in a fast-food restaurant, you tell yourself it's just to pay the bills until you become a real chef. You stay away from fatty foods and yet you found yourself going so far as to buy a ganja-infused double-chocolate brownie made with rich Trinidad cocoa. You'd bought it from the nice lady with the gap tooth in the green market. Just a small piece, she'd said. A tiny morsel of the rich, pudgy square would do. You ate the whole thing. No effect. Nothing. Not a damn thing! This is how you discover that you fall into that select category of People For Whom Ganja Is Useless.

Tonight, it's only 7.11 p.m. and already you have to make a mental note to visit Massy Stores tomorrow to pick up more beer. The last crate stands next to the fridge looking like the emptiest thing in the world. Then, the Grindr notification bleeps.

Someone with a profile called *RightNow95* is clearly not promising. Though not unusual in a country where people are still funny about these things, a blank profile is still disappointing, even if it holds out the suggestion of something quick, without frills—a casualness that borders on carelessness or sweet surrender. The thought of another hour alone listening to Taylor moan about cardigans is too much. You look at the black space where *RightNow95*'s face should be and say to yourself: who knows what lies behind the emptiness? A little chat won't hurt. You send a terse greeting in the universal opener to modern love:

What's up?

There's an instant reply:

what you doing?

Then you both go through the checklist: age, height, hair colour, eye colour, body type, preferred sexual position, penis size; can you host, in the closet, out or discrete...

Finally, you reach the make-or-break point.

pic? *RightNow95* asks.

Post-breakup depression and the extra hours of running have reshaped your body. And for this, at least, you have something to be thankful for. You're surprised by just how pleased you are with your own image. You take the photo in the bathroom mirror wearing nothing but jeans. You're not a jock, not a twink, but you've got this twunk thing going. You hit send.

RightNow95's swift reply: nice

He sends his photo. What. The. Fuck. You almost drop the phone. He's hot. Absolutely hot. He's in jeans too. He's got tattoos. Given his Latino good looks, you assume he's Venezuelan. A stolen image, surely? You vacillate between being impressed – his dreamy gaze into the camera, his washboard abs, his tussled hair – and being convinced this is some kind of sham, some dodgy catfish operation. But the image has done its work. You exchange numbers. He tells you his location. Shit, he's literally down the street. He can come over now. Right now.

Your face looks a mess. Your hair looks a mess. Your clothes look a mess. You try to slick your curls back with water from the bathroom tap. You decide the curls aren't falling with that effortless, uncultivated, everyday chaos you like. Start from scratch. You have a shower; let the water run over your head, as if being baptised; let the wet hair fall however it will as you dry off and put on another pair of blue jeans and a white t-shirt. Then you switch to black jeans and a black t-shirt. You're still not convinced you look attractive enough compared to him, but perhaps some extra daubs of cologne will help cloak your shortcomings. You guzzle Listerine. And then the thought creeps into your head. Is it too soon? Is this all too soon?

You remember the articles you read yesterday. "What to do to get over betrayal", "Learning how to love again", "The secret to being single and happy". One article, "How to move on after a breakup", listed five things to do and not to do. Fucking around was on the list of things NOT to do.

"It will be weird, you will feel guilty," author Laura Carmichael of *Modern Living* observed. Not to mention the usual fears about STDs. Shit, what about Covid? And, well, what if this really is a catfish operation and some bandit wants to rob you? In Trinidad, not unheard of.

You decide to stick to your practice of meeting people only in public. When he arrives, we'll go to the bar around the corner. That way, you decide, there will be witnesses to your interaction – at least the first part of it. There'll be people who could later say, Yes, Officer, we did see the unkempt little twunk with the wet curly hair and the other fella who looked like Juan Guaido. They came to the bar, had a few Caribs then left.

You could also text your best friend, Finn – who lives around the corner – the details known to you thus far: Mr Guaido's mobile number and his Grindr profile (though it has no details and could easily be deleted). Another message comes before you complete the thought –

fuera

He's outside.

He's *really* outside.

Keys. Wallet. You also pick up a tattered pack of spearmint gum. You pause at the door and send Finn that text with the skeleton details. Then, just so he's not caught off guard, you decide to tell the guy waiting outside your gate that you'd like to go to the bar around the corner first.

That okay?

sure

He's taller than you expect. His hair is slightly longer, sleeker and shinier, like an Instagram model's. In fact, he looks like a walking Instagram post with his luxury-brand joggers, fashionable t-shirt. All that's missing is some idyllic background like Mykonos, the California wine country, or the beaches of Mallorca. Not the subdued, sleepy streets of Woodbrook where sometimes late at night, sad prostitutes come out to get customers. As you and Mr Instagram walk to the bar, he smiles and tells you his name is Paquito and reveals a set of teeth vined with braces. The chaplet of tiny metallic brackets glisten under the streetlight. This surprise, which at once makes him appear vulnerable and vain, endears him to you. As if reading your mind, he says:

I like your curly hair

The bar's a hole in the wall with a jukebox that's never worked. Beer posters are plastered everywhere. There are no windows. Large doors open onto the pavement. The waitress says no one without a mask is allowed. You realise you've forgotten yours, though Paquito has his. You quickly turn around and exit. You've no problem with this abrupt end to the public segment of the date, at least the waiter saw you both, and too besides, there was a man on a bike who cycled past slowly, looking at you a little too intently, before you both turned the corner back to your place.

Paquito's carrying a navy Jansport knapsack, like the one your half-Venezuelan cousin, Felix, used to carry years ago. And for a moment, this coincidence makes you remember how Felix would often use his knapsack to keep his slingshot, his sneakers, maybe a pack of Ovaltine biscuits. Paquito uses his for the gym, but you can't help but go down the road of wondering what else might be inside. Let me take your bag, you say, as you shut the door behind you, once you're both indoors. He gladly relinquishes it. It's light – as light as your mood has now become. He sits on the sofa, waiting patiently for you.

After the sex, which renews your faith in the healing power of the carnal act, you spend a torturously long time telling him in broken Spanish about yourself, how you've been looking to improve your Spanish and maybe you could practice each other's mother tongue – though you really hope this involves tonguing of another kind. You don't feel bad or guilty at all. You feel as if for a moment a world of troubles has been shrunk to just two spent bodies lying side by side.

Later, with a contented look, Paquito grins as you walk him to the gate. He stops suddenly and hugs you. He starts to say something in broken English about having a really good time, then he pauses, pulls out his phone, and starts typing a note for Google to translate:

please can i have some cash to buy groceries i've no food and need oats and eggs

Of course. There had to be a catch. It was all too good from

the start – too easy, too fast. How could you be so naïve? To think
a 10 would be interested in a 6, with your grey hairs, scrawny
chicken chest, average face. Twunk my ass. Still, a part of you
begins to feel sorry for him, to think how desperate a person
must be to beg for cash for food, to use their – your mind
wanders back to the sex, then quickly flits to what you would do
if you, like him, were a foreigner in a strange land who had fled
a country ruled by a dictator. If he was desperate, what were you?
You had read of all the foreigners being robbed, murdered,
exploited. Of dead Venezuelans found in cesspits. You don't
want to think of the stories of sex work and sex trafficking.

But one thing you know for sure: there is no way you are
taking out your wallet to give this man cash. At the same time,
you also know there is the possibility – as remote as it is – that
this could just be a desperate man in need of food. This could
simply be someone for whom all options have run out. Yes,
he's wearing all these brand-name clothes, but could they be
cheap imitations? Should it even matter what he is wearing?
Should you give him the benefit of the doubt?

You work out a compromise: you will give him a few
groceries you've gathered in your pantry (before the pandemic,
you had been zealously preparing for a disaster for months, to
the chagrin of your ex-boyfriend, Dexter). But even as you
formulate this plan and tell Paquito to wait a moment you'll be
right back, something like hurt bubbles over in you. You could
never work out how to hide your feelings. Dexter always saw
through you too. Paquito says:

lo siento, i should have not asked never mind, tranquilo

And you see what looks like shame on Paquito's face. No,
you tell him. Stay here. Back inside you grab baked beans, tuna,
sardines. You add a four-pack of caramel popcorn Dexter had
bought months ago and never ate. You add some low-calorie
fruit juice Dexter also bought which you hated (he thought

you were getting too fat, what an asshole). To the bag, you include half-dozen eggs. There are two big packs of Ovaltine biscuits, so you grab one. You keep one back because you still like to eat them; they comfort you, remind you of those days in the country with Felix.

You go outside and hand Paquito the bag. His knapsack is already open, like a dog's mouth expectantly waiting. Still, you find that you are not as upset as you should be. You're disappointed in yourself but you also see a sad look on his face, which is suddenly not that handsome after all. You feel, maybe hope, that something has passed between you both—some admission of vulnerability that eclipses what has actually passed between you and this stranger. You find yourself hugging him, and for a moment, his body relaxes in your arms, which makes you feel good, feel that maybe the magic of the whole night wasn't entirely a mirage and maybe, maybe, you are wanted after all. He says:

me, you, viernes beberemos

Drinks Friday? You think not. Yes, you say aloud, nodding as if convincing yourself. You wonder if you will ever see him again.

You remember that day on the beach many years ago, when your family would spend every August in Toco. You would leave under cover of night, when it was cooler and the moon shone over the surface of the sea just beyond the winding road, as Father navigated the darkness.

That August, your cousin, Felix, joined the annual ritual with his older brother Ricardo, whom you didn't like because Ricardo would only talk to your sisters. One day on the beach, you were exploring the length of the small bay, crossing over rocks, when Felix discovered a giant gash in the cliff. It tunnelled, darkly, through the land to a hidden cove.

Smooth white stones lined this cove. It seemed filled only with exotic creatures unknown to man. There was a small stream that emptied into the sea, its water cutting across a sandy area of the beach, making fans like tiny deltas. You remember Felix telling you the names and uses of various plants and creatures, telling you about his dream of one day becoming a forest ranger, sometimes speaking to you in Spanish, and at one point boasting how his Spanish was way better than yours. Then, he abruptly takes off his trunks, flashing you. Let's take a dip, he says, mischief in his eyes.

You had seen your Father naked before, but the fact of Father's maleness had never really registered. It was like any other piece of furniture back at home in the city: reliable, functional, taken for granted. But Felix is so different yet so similar. What shocks you is the surprisingly vulnerable pink tip of it, how it perfectly matches the pink of his lips. And now you wonder if all males have such hidden patterns and secrets, including the men you sometimes stare at every August on the beach with their goatees and fluorescent board shorts. Do you like them, you wonder. *He* makes you wonder.

Perhaps there was something about the hotness of the little wooden house amid the sleepy trees. Perhaps it was the wall of sound that surrounded the house – the crickets chirping, the sea gulls crying, the wind rustling through the broad leaves of the breadfruit trees. Perhaps it was the gentle way the house exhaled, the bones of its structure crackling and contracting as the night cooled. Or perhaps it was just how close Felix liked to be to you, the nearness of his hot limbs, the soapy smell of his flesh. Maybe it was all of this that made you fall into a spell that same night after skinny dipping with him. Maybe it was the way he casually touched your thigh as he lay next to you on the mattress on the floor whispering a story in the cosy room.

Maybe it was the story he told you, in graphic detail, about having sex with a girl named Jasmine – a girl you're not even sure exists – as he takes your cock in his hands. You haven't even noticed how hard you've become until you register the shock of his hands, hands that are the same as yours yet not the same. Fingers firm yet compliant; soft yet sovereign. You feel a small ooze of fluid pearl at the tip of your dick. And, as he whispers and whispers and whispers into your ear, his tongue so close, you feel something building, some wave about to crash, but he stops just at that point when the truth would be too messy.

It never happens again. You never speak to Felix about the night he stroked your dick, he never mentions it either. It is as if it never happened. But you know that for you it has changed everything. There is a truth inside you now, a truth you are finally willing to reckon with, a truth as taboo as what you had done. It is something you will never forget as you both move on from that August – you studying hard at the Hospitality Institute to achieve your dream of becoming a chef in a Michelin-star restaurant; Felix immersing himself in life in Paramin, becoming a jab jab, then a blue devil, liming with the fellas in the village, starting a tiny business selling jewellery made from seeds.

Dexter messages you on Friday. You already know what he wants even before you read the message. He wants to pick up a few things he's left at the apartment.

You've already assembled his things, have them in a neat pile on the table near to the door. These last few months, these items have been riling you, each taking you back to a time when he hadn't yet dumped you for a younger model named Duane, whom he met at the gym.

There is the lamp with the weird lampshade that he thought

was "youthful" and "arty" and bought without consulting you, placing it on your nightstand. Then, the giant paperweight he brought home from the law firm he worked at even though it was the ugliest thing you ever saw – some kind of mutant turtle. There was his old Igbo mask that scared the fuck out of you at nights. And an ancient CD player with an equally ancient CD collection (he had a weakness for Celine Dion, Luther Vandross, and various opera singers like Jessye Norman and Kiri Te Kanawa).

As you wait for him to arrive, staring at these spiteful relics, you find yourself glimpsing the pack of Ovaltine biscuits. You text Finn, tell him all about Paquito and what happened that night. The reply is quick:

What?! No way, that's super sketchy. Avoid. Avoid like the plague...

You put down the phone. You munch an Ovaltine biscuit. You'll get started on dinner soon. At least that's one thing you will always be able to do no matter what. Cook yourself some love.

But first you find yourself browsing Facebook. Your feed is filled with stuff your ex-classmates from the Hospitality Institute are doing.

Someone is experimenting with macarons. Another is trying out all sorts of fancy cakes and pastries. The avalanche of sweetbreads and savoury rolls paints a picture that brings on a sick realisation: other people are moving on with life, making plans, sharing their hopes and dreams.

You are about to scroll on to something else when you see one of your friends' most recent photograph, a throwback to a few months ago, apparently taken at a hair salon on Alfredo Street. In the photo is Paquito, standing with a hair dryer.

In this moment, the phantom of Paquito has become real. In the caption your friend complains about not having her hair done in months. Paquito is not tagged, not named. But at least you know for sure now he is a hairdresser. Maybe he's legit. Maybe he was truly in dire straits. Hairdressers, too, are now shut down because of the pandemic. Could it really be? Was it really real?

You begin to text him. You wonder what to say. No, don't. Don't bother. You don't want to seem desperate. You browse dating websites for advice on seeming cool. "Definitely don't message too early," Lucinda Cocklehurst of *Good Company* says. It's been three days, so that's okay, you think.

"If you've previously set a tentative plan, it's okay to bring that up," counters Fred Fox in *Glitz* and that line alone is the validation you need. He did say Friday, you think. Maybe he could really help you with your Spanish? You have wanted to learn more, after all. You remember reading how Spanish is the world's most popular language, except for Mandarin. You pull up Google and start researching random Spanish phrases:

How was your day?	*¿Que tal tu día?*
What are you up to?	*¿Que piensas hacer?*
I want your cock.	*Quiero tu polla.*

No, don't. You put the phone down and start preparing dinner. Get a grip, you say. This is the real world; things don't happen like this. Hustlers don't become husbands. Do you think this is *Pretty Woman*?

And fuck Michelin stars and macarons and puff pastries, tonight you just want some thick steak fries and a hamburger. You gather your ingredients, moving through your small but well-stocked kitchen. Your parents have been helping you with groceries, the same groceries you handed over the other night so magnanimously. Funny how after everything, you've reverted back to where you started. Mother and Father. You shudder at the thought of moving back home. As you slice into an onion, Dexter arrives. He's still got keys, you remember with annoyance.

The conversation bristles the way conversations do when they occur between two people who have recently broken up. In such conversations, "Hello" might as well be "You have some gall showing your face here, you bastard"; "Would you like to have a seat?" becomes "I bought this couch, bitch, and I am keeping it"; "Well, it's getting late" means "Get the fuck out".

Dexter has come from after-work drinks with the partners. In his shirt and tie, he veers from being sheepishly awkward, to having a look of cool malice and spite, like a senior corporate villain in a Michael Mann movie. He thanks you for gathering his things, slowly places them into the box he's walked with, and then gives you a reminder to send him the cash you owe him for the last electricity bill he had unilaterally taken upon himself to pay some time before the breakup. Sure, you say, wishing you could sign a cheque right now but secretly relishing the thought of never repaying him. Then, he notices you're cooking.

How's the dream of becoming a chef going these days? Dexter says.

For a moment you're not sure if there's mocking sarcasm in his voice. Is he now, after everything that he has done to you with that little gym rat, mocking your dream? You always felt he looked down on your goals, with his corporate law background; that he always felt they were too menial, you were too menial. Or is his question mocking the way life has a way of bringing people down from their dreams? Is he commiserating? Either way, something tastes bitter. You are about to say, What the fuck is it to you? Instead, you say, It's Friday and it's getting late and Duane must be waiting.

Dexter has a look of disappointment, which almost hurts you as much as everything else, as though, with your words, you've put the final nail in the coffin of something.

It's over.

It's really and truly over.

When he leaves, you put a burger patty on the fire, the oil spits and spatters violently as the raw meat sizzles. The nearby toaster heats up and the sesame seed buns get crisp. You top the patties with huge slices of cheese and throw on mushrooms. On the bun, you bathe everything with mayonnaise and ketchup and mustard. You open a bottle of pickles. You add the steak fries, which you've cooked in the oven despite your better judgment, and slather them with garlic sauce. And then you sit and watch your Pollock masterpiece on the plate. Despite how hungry you are, you can't eat. You feel it coming.

The tears.

You pick up your phone. Against your better judgment, but with a distress that feels familiar, you send a message to Paquito and await the reply:

| Come over tonight, | *Ven esta noche,* |
| I cooked a meal for you. | *te preparé una comida.* |

About an hour later, around 9 pm, Paquito's reply comes. He says he's in Chaguanas but is on his way back to Woodbrook and could come over later to eat something.

You quickly fry a second burger. You need more rings, so you slice into an onion. As you slice, the knife slips, you nick your finger. Out of a very small cut, a river of blood flows and flows and you wonder how so much blood could come from so tiny a wound. In the bathroom you wash your hands and apply a bandage, look at yourself in the mirror and doubt what you see is really standing before you.

When the second burger is done, you put all the food away in the microwave.

You wait.

You wait.

Towards midnight, you are ravenous, but you decide to give it one more hour.

You wait. He might still come, you think.

You wait.

1960

Port of Spain, April 22, 1960

It was my mistake. I was the one who thought courting Maisie would make things different, would get people to stop whispering. We went out a couple of times. Soon we became the talk of the typing pool, which annoyed me. Maisie was choice and all the fellas wanted details. Her kisses were wet. Whenever we went to dinner she'd rub her feet against the inside of my thigh. When I couldn't take it any more, I started to hide in the bathroom stalls at work during the lunch break. I didn't want to have to speak to anyone.

I had to get out. I had to end it with Maisie and quit the job.

On our last date, Maisie started crying because I'd turned up drunk again. She ran down the street away from our rendezvous, which was outside Globe. I went into the cinema. I bought a ticket for the matinee. I sat in the dark, smoked, and waited. The matinee was a film starring Brigitte Bardot called *The Truth*. There were wolf whistles whenever Bardot appeared onscreen. I tried but I couldn't read the blurry subtitles, so I got up to leave, stepping on someone's foot on the way out. He held my wrist and said *Howdy* in this suggestive way and wouldn't let go of me, as though he recognised me from somewhere and wanted something from me. I made to pull away. But he held on tighter. I gave in. I sat down next to him. He smelled of cigars and rum. He never let go of my hand, rubbing it against the fabric of his twill trousers. Beneath the fabric, I could feel his thick muffler. When we and the film finished, I got up and walked out of the cinema into the white glare.

After the whole Maisie affair, I decided I'd take a room on French Street to be closer to my new job and to get away from downtown. I was starting on Monday and needed a new suit. My landlady said there was a tailor around the corner, and I thought that a stroke of good luck. I was starting afresh. I could put everything, all of it, behind me.

I remember thinking it might be busy because it's Friday, but there was nobody around. There's just the tailor who sits as though he's been waiting for me all day. He's wearing a stylish Cab Calloway suit with a long chain dangling between his legs. His father had been a tailor too, he says, and worked in this same spot. That makes me smile. Then, it makes me glum. It's a stuffy, two-room space at the side of an old rotten house. Everything smells musty and left behind. All around are rolls of fabric and swatches of flannels, mohairs, Madras plaids. There is an old, battered sign on the wall, probably his father's. It says:

TAILOR and CUTTER
Suits made to Order
Popular and Competitive Prices

He needs ten measurements from me to make the suit. First, the jacket: collar to waist-length, sleeve, half back, chest, and waist. Then, the trouser: waist, seat, outside leg, inside leg, and the cuff. I feel him wrap the tape up, down, in front and behind me, as though he's a Lilliputian and I'm Gulliver. Sometimes he puts his finger between my body and the tape for leeway. Occasionally he pauses, puts the tape around his neck so that it dangles like a thin snake, goes to a table and writes measurements in a notebook with a pencil, like the Bookman recording sins. When he's ready to do my inside leg, he pinches and pulls up his trousers. He kneels. I notice he's a good-looking guy. He has a square jaw, symmetrical face, and sultry eyes with long eyelashes. He places his face right in front my crotch, guides the tape up to the apex between my legs. Then, he uses his long index finger to press the tape onto me. Light but certain is his touch, like a feather being trailed over your skin. His other fingers graze me, ever so slightly. He looks up at me. I feel something electric. I need air. I push him away. I go into the backroom. It is dark. I can make out a door, an exit of some kind. There is a small window with jalousies. I look outside the window into a courtyard filled with pots of Spanish thyme. He chuckles as though accustomed to my reaction.

Come back for it next week, he says. That smile.

I've changed my mind, I say. I can't afford this.

I leave him standing there.

I go to Ariapita Avenue. I think of going to London Theatre to watch another film but it's too early. I take the trolley bus into town.

I'm walking along Park Street when I see a man come out of Globe. We look at one another on cue, as if we're in some kind of Western. He doesn't look like the man from last time. This man is Portuguese-looking. He's immaculately dressed in a white linen suit and wears a superior hat. He's got a debonair quality about him. He is tall and his svelte body stands sharp against everything else around him. He has this relaxed, direct way of looking at you that suggests he's got money. We are side by side, walking in the same direction. I let him take the lead. I slow down a little. Several times he looks over his shoulder at me. I want to end this game. I want to go somewhere else.

But I decide to follow him.

We end up in a drinking saloon in a cheap hotel on Charlotte Street. He holds open the door, as if to say *After you*. The room is filled with cigarette smoke and little groups of men riotous with drink. I hear the knock of billiard boards in an adjoining room. In less than half hour we've gulped five drinks each. I feel like someone else has entered my body. I am someone else.

I've got tickets for a concert while I'm in town, he says. Would you like to join me?

I'm too drunk for a show right now, I say.

He flashes a big, wide, perfect smile, then says: It's not today, it's tomorrow.

What are we going to do until then? I say.

I'm sure we can find a way to spend the time, he says. Something between us, if not already confirmed, has been cemented.

What about your wife? I say, as I point to the wedding ring on his finger. Wouldn't you prefer to go to the show with her?

She doesn't come with me on my trips to Port of Spain, he says.

I see, I say.

We're having fun together you and I, no? he says. Come to the concert. We'll have dinner after.

I might have church or something, I say.

He laughs. Meet me outside Globe again, he says.

Outside, the harsh white light of the street begins to fade to something soft and blue. The room's gotten much louder, more crowded. I scarf my scotch. I've never made plans with a guy like this ahead of time. Everything that's happened, has just happened. That's just how it's been. Everything I've taken, I've taken because I could. Then moved on. This won't be any different. I know it won't.

I nod yes to his request to meet tomorrow.

Great, see you at seven, he says. We can eat after the show.

Meanwhile, how can we finish off this evening? He looks at me as if he's digging deep inside me, while also playing around in his own head. I know, he finally says. Let's go take a dip.

Sure, but where? I say.

Next thing I know we're in the street again. Then, we find his car, cut out of town, and burn down the highway. He drives a blue Chevrolet, one of the 1959 models. He opens a bottle of rum with his teeth and passes it to me. Wind blows through my hair like revolution. We go faster and faster and faster and it's all too much. I lean over the side of the car, retch and vomit. He laughs. But I feel much better.

When we get to Carenage, we strip and bathe naked. The sea is calm. I splash about in the seawater. It gets into my nostrils, it gets into my throat. It revives me. He swims out far. I follow him.

He drops me back to my room that night. Alone in my bed, I'm still swimming.

Port of Spain, April 23, 1960

At dawn, I hear the city corporation men scraping up rubbish outside. In the garden next door, macaws and parrots are making noises. The light in my room is bright and hot. My head feels light.

His card with his number sits on my bedside table. But I've no phone. I've no way of letting him know I'm not coming to meet him. I never was. He'll get the point when I don't show up.

Today, I need to sort out my room. It's smaller and a lot cheaper than the last, but I don't mind starting over. That's what I've always done. There's not much to look at: no paintings, no plants, no fancy furniture. Just a shabby little cabinet whose doors don't close properly, a bedside table with a bloated lamp on it, and a mottled, full-length mirror that doubles the sadness of the empty space. I've moved around with this mirror for years. Sometimes, I look into it and feel as though the reflection belongs to other people: people I've left behind, people at my old jobs, people in the street, people I'm yet to meet.

I scrub the floors. I rearrange the furniture. The new arrangement isn't much of an improvement in the small space. I'm shaky all day and I can't tell if it's because I've got the zings from last night or what. I have half a bottle of scotch by the bed and feel bad because I know that's not likely to be enough to keep me home all afternoon. I have some shots and look into the mirror and stare at my round face, my large eyes, my reddish lips, my broad shoulders. I play around a bit, stand taller, stand firmer, try to find who I should be.

Downtown, I pass a bar twice before deciding to try to go in. Luckily, they let me in. I'm relieved. These days, it's hard to remember which establishments have banned me and which have not. I have more shots. I play pool. I smoke.

And then I begin to wonder. What show was he talking about? Probably some calypso thing. Then, a fight breaks out and someone calls for the police and I figure it's best to make a move, though I'm not sure where I should go next. I tool around. I think of heading to 55 Queen Street, where there's always something going on, but, somehow, I'm not in the mood.

Then, I figure it's no use fighting.

I start walking to Park Street.

I get there early, at six, and he's already there, parked up in the Chevrolet. He's wearing another fine suit, this time grey. He smells of a cologne I recognise, Aramis, the one I used to sell in the department store on Frederick Street. Its notes are a splash of seawater.

So what's this show about? I say.

It's a surprise, he says. He smiles. But I'm worried. I don't like many things, but most of all I don't like surprises.

We drive north through the city then, around the Savannah. We pass the little castle that looks like a giant dollhouse. I wonder if I'll ever meet the people who live in that house. Then, he turns off the road and I realise where we're heading.

I'm not dressed for Queen's Hall, I say.

You look fine, he says. He puts his hand on my knee.

In the lobby everyone stares. They look at me, then they look at him, incredulous, which angers me.

Inside the hall, we have seats near the middle. I read the programme. It says simply: "MARIAN ANDERSON – QUEEN'S HALL". Inside, a notice says the concert is under the patronage of Lord and Lady Hailes. The lights suddenly dim and then there's a hush. The curtains open.

She emerges from the wings, wearing a large black taffeta gown. There is a diamond broach on her lapel that reflects rainbow light all over the auditorium. She begins with Haydn's 'The Spirit's Song', a song that creeps up and startles me. Her voice is both heavy and light, plaintive and joyful. Her notes engulf me like his strong cologne. She sings Haydn, Mozart, Schubert, Tchaikovsky. There's an intermission. I grab a glass of wine from one of the waiters and feel the heat of all the people staring again. When the concert continues, I feel uncomfortable in our warm seats. She sings 'Lullaby' and 'Dreamin''. Then she sings 'None But the Lonely Heart' and 'My Mother Bids Me Bind My Hair'. When she sings 'Softly Awakes My Heart' from *Samson and Delilah,* it feels like a record is playing and playing and I'm spinning and spinning. He touches my thigh with the tip of his little finger. His cologne is too much. This is too much. The chromatic piano music, her steely voice, they are too much. Her soaring and aching for something in the clouds, it is all too much, too romantic, too beautiful, too unlike anything I've ever heard or experienced. It feels like too cruel a glimpse at some dream I know will never come true. I am under-dressed. They are staring at us. They are all staring at us.

Samson, she belts out at the song's climax, *Samson, I love you!*

Some knife stabs me. I can't take it anymore. Which is why I do what I do next.

She is singing her last song, 'Adieu' when I get up and walk out.

Under the trees outside, I crumple his card. I pelt it to the ground. I don't look back.

St Clair, July 15, 1979

Maisie is in the garden again. From our kitchen I see her. She bows before the ginger lilies like a worshipper bowing at a mosque. I have another cup of coffee. Sunday mornings like this are made for coffee. The room fills with its scent: cedar, charcoal, chocolate and walnut. The kitchen needs to be renovated, I think. I used to like the colourful Mexican tiles the house came with, but now they look dated. I've always wanted something a little more modern. But somehow, after all these years, we've just never gotten round to changing things up. I step back to the window and look at Maisie again. Now she's attacking some weeds that have grown up around the flowers.

Alana starts to blast loud music from her room upstairs. It's something instrumental, something operatic.

A fine contralto, a voice I recognise.

It's *that* voice.

Dad, isn't she amazing? Alana says as I open her bedroom door. Someone mentioned her at choir practice yesterday. She was the first African-American to perform at the Met Opera. Apparently she once came to Trinidad and sang at Queen's Hall!

I know, I say. I was there.

What? That's amazing, she says. What was it like?

I was young, I say. I don't really remember. It was a long time ago. Could you turn down the volume a bit? I think I have a little headache.

I leave her listening. I shut the door and head to the garden to help Maisie uproot the weeds.

SELECTED BOYS: 2013-2016

Manuel

They started to make out in front of me. The younger guy took off his shirt. He had tight abs and Teen Wolf tattoos. His nipples were copper coins you wanted to collect.

I tried to get in between them. But each time, they danced around me. The younger guy started to take off his trousers. Geoffrey was already naked. He lifted the younger guy, heaved him onto the bed and helped him peel off the moult of his jeans until it was a denim waterfall crumpled on the floor. I looked at the younger guy lying there with his trendy haircut looking perfectly at ease, more perfectly at ease than I'd ever be in a situation like this, and everything in me deflated. I stepped back. I switched on Geoffrey's stereo. It was Carnival time. I found something simple, something pulsing, something up-tempo like we played every day at the gym – it was the latest soca by Super Blue & The Love Band. But 'Fantastic Friday' wasn't enough to drown my thoughts that kept popping up like mushrooms after rain. I'd do anything for Geoffrey, I said to myself, over and over as I watched him put on a condom and slather lube on his cock, a cock that was now incredibly eager as it curved to a destination that didn't include me, a destination that, tonight, was this other guy's seemingly perfect, irresistible hole. I sat on the armchair. I watched as the other guy positioned himself. Geoffrey propped his butt up with a pillow then got him to bend his knees so that the guy's feet were flat against Geoffrey's chest. Geoffrey entered him slowly at first, then he rammed him for what seemed like forever, without so much as glancing in my direction, all as Super Blue and company thumped from the speakers, singing: *The bouncing start, the bouncing start, the bouncing start*...

I'd do anything for Geoffrey. But this?

Hakeem

Weeks later, Easter time.

I tried to take off my shirt, but my arm got stuck. I hit the other dude in the face. Then Geoffrey tripped over his Buddha sculpture and fell flat on the floor and both of us – me and the other guy – moved to help him but we butt our heads together so hard we had to rest for a bit.

Geoffrey brought out the joints he kept for emergencies. After a few hits, we got back in the mood. I rubbed up against the other dude's ass. I got hard. I said:

This is GREAT, so GREAT!

The dude turned around and I saw he had long dimples and pretty Billy Zane eyes. We kissed. I sucked on his Julie mango lips. When Geoffrey saw this, he grabbed my cock and towed me away from the guy towards him. Then, it was Geoffrey's turn to kiss the guy. He sailed between us like a ship gliding into port, all the while never letting go of my shaft, which made me feel like he was holding on to me – showing me that he would not leave me. But then, he kissed the guy and really got into it and though he still wrapped his fingers around my base, he didn't seem to be into it so much anymore. I stroked the other guy's arm and the Julie mango lips returned to me and we went around like this for a while taking turns: me kissing Geoffrey, Geoffrey kissing the guy, the guy kissing me.

At length, we decided to move things to the sofa because the wind chimes were getting distracting (it was a gusty night). But the sofa was too small. Geoffrey would often correct me; say it was a love seat. I felt thwarted when he and the guy ended up on it together. Out of pique, I climbed on the coffee table and loomed over the guy's head, letting my dick fall in front his face like a caraille swaying from a vine. He wanted to suck it, but I turned it to Geoffrey. I knew Geoffrey wouldn't take it. We'd been together a year now and he had never taken it. He was an exclusive top, he would say. This bothered me. Was he ashamed? Was he afraid? Did he secretly judge me because I was the passive partner? Geoffrey turned away from the belligerent club of my penis and resumed his one-on-one tongue session with the guy. Then the love seat fell over and I felt equilibrium had finally been restored. Until, that is, our dog came into the room looking like a gremlin and pounced on the guy and Geoffrey got mad because it was my job to crate Desdemona.

You can't do one simple task, Duane? he yelled.

That ruined it for me and I could tell it had also been ruined for Geoffrey. He often snapped at me in a tone that seemed to say *I'm fed up with you*. He would almost immediately apologise and say things like *No, of course I love you* or *I'm just under a lot of stress at the bank* or *I'm becoming a grumpy old man*. I'd convince myself it was all nothing, that I was imagining things. I should really stop second guessing him, I'd say; I need to stop overthinking. We had problems. We had misunderstandings. There were differences between us. But we also had love. And we were doing the work. We were making it work.

Tonight though, Geoffrey said nothing by way of apology.

But that might have been because the other dude was still eager, still wanted to give it a go and had started to suck and slurp enthusiastically on our limp dicks, playing, licking, blowing on them with his warm breath, trying to reignite what had been alive moments before.

Jameson

I knew we definitely weren't going to fuck this guy when Geoffrey started asking him about his name.

So you mean your parents named you after a brand of whiskey? Geoffrey said.

Jameson, whom we'd picked up at a Boycode party, looked at Geoffrey as though Geoffrey had stabbed him. He was wearing a blue dip-dye t-shirt that clung to his torso. He had a scar on the side of his face that reminded me of Mufasa's brother in *The Lion King* (I always thought Scar was hot). In the dim of our living room, Jameson's eyes pooled into black, sparkling lakes.

Why'd you have to be so rude? I asked Geoffrey after Jameson gathered his things and left without a word.

Didn't you want to know, too? Geoffrey said. That whiskey's not *that* great.

I laughed and Geoffrey cuddled me and started singing something by the Mighty Sparrow because that's what he did whenever he got tipsy. On these nights, whenever our adventures didn't pan out and it ended up being just the two of us, it was easy to remember this was why I was with him.

We didn't meet at the gym, where I had met all my previous boyfriends. We met in the bookstore on the other side of the plaza. Geoffrey worked in the bank branch across the road. I was drifting among the canyons of book stacks, and he yelped when he saw me.

Sorry, he'd said as he came over, trying to seem cool. You startled me. Nobody's ever in the poetry section.

I hadn't noticed I was in the poetry section; it was so small. I was taking a class in management at the Open Campus and had gone to find a textbook but got distracted by the self-help titles like *The Top Ten Habits of Successful People* and *How to Find Love in 100 Days* and *The Power of Saying No*. I was hoping to become manager at the gym, which suddenly struck me as a rather unintellectual ambition as I stared into Geoffrey's handsome, bespectacled, poetry-loving face. He was a banker for sure, wearing a charcoal grey suit, a blue oxford shirt with mother-of-pearl buttons, and a gold tie. He said he was looking for a birthday present for one of his friends.

I was intrigued by his love of books (he said it wasn't odd for a banker to be interested in poetry, hadn't T.S. Eliot been a bank clerk after all?) The first time I slept over at his place, he showed me the colourful spines of all the titles in his library. He pulled down a slim volume by a poet who'd written about gyms, and this fascinated me because I'd never thought anyone might find anything poetic about my world; a world of protein shakes and sweat stains and men grunting as soca and American pop music played on loop.

When we were alone after Jameson left, it was easy to fall back into memories of those early months together, going out for dinners at The Verandah, seeing films like *Amour*, attending plays and literary festivals. It was easy to believe that maybe I had finally found someone – and God knows I'd been trying to find someone – and he was just for me. It was easy to forget, or perhaps wilfully ignore, all that was overtaking us. That night, I still felt high from the Boycode party, but Geoffrey said he felt tired and didn't want to have sex, so we lay in bed, his salt and pepper head resting on my shoulder, as small frogs sang outside. I felt a pang of regret because Jameson had the best bubble butt I'd ever seen – and I'd seen a lot – and a part of me thought it might have been nice to do more than kiss him on a smoky dance floor, as Geoffrey and I had done earlier that night, dancing to 'Carnival Tabanca' by Bunji. There had been so many gorgeous men at the party, with great muscles and classy shirts, all eying me, all eying both of us. I could have had any one of them, I thought, but only Geoffrey had me because he was the one who really saw me, who believed in my goals, as modest as they were, who did things like recite 'At the Gym' by Mark Doty knowing it would inspire me. Without even being conscious of it, blood rushed to my dick, and I became unrelentingly hard. I played with Geoffrey's nipples to see if he might wake, but he continued to sleep, a little bit of his drool falling onto my chest. I tried to join him in slumber but I kept hearing soca, kept seeing smoke and lights from the dancefloor, the gaudy Christmas decorations on the bar, the topless bartenders in Santa hats, kept thinking of Jameson and his bubble butt.

Dexter

I didn't like Geoffrey's friends because I was pretty sure none of them liked me. Which was why I was shocked when Geoffrey told me one night that Dexter wanted to come over.

This is your Valentine's Day surprise? I asked.

Maybe if it's with someone we *both* know you'll like it better? Geoffrey said.

I threw up a little inside because I'd never told Geoffrey I didn't like his friends. Whenever we limed they'd always bring up the fact that I was from La Puerta, as though that made me less than them. Once, not long after we'd started dating, Lystra,

Geoffrey's other lawyer friend who owned Mendonca & Mendonca, interrogated me about how old I was and where I'd met him and what my intentions were. Dexter would call Geoffrey my sugar daddy, though I made a point of always paying my way. This friend in particular had a manner of keeping people distant by making passive-aggressive remarks.

I see you've been working out, Dexter said as he came in. I don't blame you. You've got nothing else to do at that gym.

The three of us sat in the living room, each on a separate piece of furniture. On the wall behind us were the drawings I'd done of old gingerbread houses all over Woodbrook, drawings Geoffrey had insisted on framing with expensive museum glass.

The three of us chatted about whether Ebola might make it to Trinidad. Geoffrey poured his favourite Casal Garcia wine. Dexter lit a du Maurier and looked at me intently.

He fucked me as Geoffrey watched and I knew then for sure Dexter had liked me all along. That knowledge of him – a knowledge that entered me through the way he held my cock as though it were precious to him, the way he traced his fingers along my Adonis belt, the way he licked my ears, the way he stared into my eyes – that knowledge of his vulnerability frightened and exhilarated me. I lay on my back, my legs wrapped around Dexter's waist, my prick hard like a green fig, rubbing against his stomach as his cock drilled deeper and deeper into me, past my second sphincter, in search of something he wanted to find in me.

Hours after, I could still taste his nicotine. I could smell his intoxicating cologne.

I told Geoffrey we shouldn't try Dexter again.

Kyle

Our experiments to revive our love life didn't always involve threesomes. One August night, after dinner at a restaurant, I wanted to lime but Geoffrey said he was tired. I could stay out.

You young fellas have too much stamina, he said, adjusting the pink rosary beads that hung from his rear-view mirror.

The remark was loaded. Geoffrey was the one who had suggested we have an open relationship. He was eight years older and he was worried he couldn't satisfy me. I had told him it didn't matter. Lots of couples have energy levels that don't match, I said. But Geoffrey was always insecure. He was insecure about my age. He was insecure about where I worked. He was sure one day I'd move on to a younger, fitter guy. He'd often tell me I was young and was still figuring myself out, still learning what worked for me and what didn't. And maybe one day, when I was seeing a little clearer, my life wouldn't include him. I might be young, I'd tell him, but I knew enough to know all relationships require compromise. Who was he to tell me what compromise was one compromise too much? After several protracted arguments – which felt like negotiations between two nation-states – I told Geoffrey I'd sleep with other people but only if he was involved. That's how it began.

Tonight, though, there was a look on Geoffrey's face that said he had made up his mind about something.

I met Kyle in Shakers. He had perfect white teeth that glowed as if under a perpetual UV light.

I know you from somewhere, he shouted over the 90s grunge music. I couldn't tell if this was a pick-up line or if it was true because the island was small. Then he remembered: You're the guy from the Ellerslie gym!

After a while, the whiskey I ordered began to do its work,

cutting a warm channel through the centre of my body. I told Kyle all about the situation with Geoffrey.

He can't believe that someone like me would be with someone like him, I said. Which is so ironic because I feel the same about him! People treat me like a piece of meat. But not Geoffrey. He sees me, you know?

Kyle listened intently, as though he'd known us both for years, patting my shoulder sympathetically.

Sex really doesn't mean *that* much, I continued, downing another whiskey.

Hours later, we went to Kyle's place. He lived in St James, not far from the Police Barracks. The houses on his street slept behind walls that were too high. He lived with his mom, but she was away. There was a picture of Jesus in the living room. Kyle lit a scented candle in his bedroom, and I noticed his giant Patrice Roberts poster. We kissed and then stripped and I noticed our shadows flickering on the wall. Kyle had a punk-rock vibe about him, but when he was naked, he was beautiful. He had one of those bodies you see on Trinidadian sprinters, lithe but rugged. He climbed up on his bed and lay on his stomach, resting his head on his folded arms. His languidness was calming. I played with his ass, probing him with one, then two fingers. The realisation that I was about to top someone for the first time in a long time sent a trickle of precum out my dick. He handed me a condom, one of those free ones you got when you did an HIV test at the Family Planning Association. He had this lube, silicone-based, that felt luxurious and extra slippery. When I inserted the tip of my cock, he gasped, asked me to pause for a moment as the pain subsided, then relaxed and told me to go ahead. Gradually, he took in all nine inches of me, so that I could bury myself to the balls, and it felt good to feel my hipbone slam against his narrow, muscular butt. I hooked my arm beneath his neck and pulled his face closer to mine – like you see all the beefy jocks do in porn – and kissed him deeply. His unfamiliar body started to feel familiar. It was as though we were liquid streaming into each other, as though we'd done this yesterday and the day before that, and I'd known this man, his silken insides, all my life. Afterwards, as we lay together, I could hear the quiet of the streets outside. A dog barked. I felt the world had changed.

The next day at his house in Fairways, I told Geoffrey I topped a guy. He said he was happy I was happy. Then, he made coffee and read the papers. Maybe this open thing could work, I thought.

Eddie

Geoffrey was making pancakes one morning when he said he'd hooked up with a guy the night before.

Will you see him again?

I don't know, he said.

I got him to give me a few details. I looked up this Eddie guy on social media. He worked at the Ministry of Labour as some kind of clerk. He had a flashy red Nissan that he had jacked up. He wore smart clothes, smarter clothes than I had ever had, which he even wore in selfies taken in his car. I pictured him worshipping Geoffrey's thick cock.

The bits of blueberry pancake in my mouth became bitter.

One week later, I told Kyle we had to stop fucking. And I told Geoffrey he had to stop seeing Eddie.

The open relationship experiment was over.

S—

Not long after, Geoffrey said he wanted to go on vacation. He
booked us on a two-week Caribbean cruise. There were loads of
hot men. At nights, after dinner, when we hung out in one of the
bars, he would point out how many prospects there were and
would ask, with solemn gravity, if I was sure about no longer
wanting to keep things open. I would interpret this as a test, say
yes, I was sure. What was love if not commitment to one person
and one person alone? I knew some people said things like: *The
will is strong but the flesh is weak*, but what did they know? If there
was one thing I had to sacrifice to keep what I had with Geoffrey
– charming, funny, caring, intelligent Geoffrey – it was all worth
it. I filled our itinerary to the max. We had jerk chicken and Red
Stripe in Jamaica. We saw the Pitons of St Lucia. We walked El
Malecón in Havana. Sipped rum in Barbados. Took pretty
pictures in Curaçao. Whenever we got back onboard the ship,
we'd be so tired we'd fall asleep in our bunks (we slept separately
because of Geoffrey's sleep apnea).

After the cruise, when we were safely back on dry land, we
saw every major cinema release. Had long discussions about
the island's politics. We cooked too much food. We had some
of my long-neglected friends over. We saw all the art exhibi-
tions. We went to all the plays. We attended all the concerts.

I focused on work at the gym. There was an opening for me
as assistant manager. Other staff in the gym had come and
gone. But I was steadfast. I was loyal. I was disciplined. All I had
to do was maintain course.

Things were going fine until the fete. It was Carnival time
again. Geoffrey's friends said they missed him. They pined for
the days when they'd all attend the same parties every year.
They missed these traditions from what they called BD: Before
Duane.

It was a cooler fete in the Oval so you had to bring drinks. I made a vat of my favourite cocktail – a Dark & Stormy with dark Guyana rum, Jamaican Ginger Wine, and lemon. I offered the group. Everyone looked at me sceptically and declined. Except Geoffrey.

I left them and went closer to the stage to see Kes the Band perform. Destra Garcia sang 'Lucy', and Machel Montano followed her, belting out 'Like a Boss'. I jumped up and down in a mosh pit that formed. At one point I looked behind me. I couldn't see Geoffrey and the group. I felt lost.

Did he tell me his name? What was it?

Sean?

Shane?

I'd fallen over at the toilets. He'd helped me up and took me to get air outside. We went to a doubles stand nearby and ate. And suddenly, everything that was hazy and woozy was all very clear.

I had tried so hard to deny so much.

My relationship just wasn't working.

We made out leaning against his car. He unzipped my fly, and my cock rushed out, liberated. He sucked it, and it was the first time in months I'd felt the sensation of soft flesh plush against my shaft, felt the hot intimacy and pressure of a wet, eager mouth, felt like someone was willing to take me – in all senses – in my entirety within them, without precondition, with no hang-ups about who was the top and who was the bottom or who was older and who was wiser or who would die first or who would stop loving first or who would be the one to end things because we were so different. From the fete in the distance, I could hear someone singing a soca about falling and I felt like I was that singer's dulcet voice, climbing a staircase of clouds into the night sky.

When I came, I felt I had cried all over him.

Dexter

It was months after I became manager of the gym. I was doing my evening rounds on the floor when Dexter came in. He started chatting with me. He couldn't decide if he wanted annual membership or something less committed. He seemed overdressed in the way people new to the gym always were. He was wearing a brand new white headband, a white t-shirt and white shorts which showed off his surprisingly toned legs. His cologne filled the room. I made a mental note to ask him what it was.

Maybe I should just do one of these spin classes, he said, they're easy, right?

A few minutes later, he fell off his bike in the class, which happens to lots of first-timers. I had to help him to his car. We laughed. A warm breeze blew through the car park. The sun had set. The sky was purple and comforting.

I hadn't been with anyone since Kyle had migrated (I'd broken up with Geoffrey a while ago now). It felt good to feel Dexter's body against mine. To feel the heaviness of him that was like a weight you might choose to push to the sky. When he drove off, I was afraid. But also happy. Maybe another era was about to start. Maybe I was ready. I went inside and finished my rounds.

People never stacked the weights in the correct order. Someone put the 30-pound dumbbell where the 20-pound one should be. The 40-pound was missing. There was a salt stain halo on the bench press. Men would lay their heads there to push muscles that had to be torn in order to grow.

I signed Dexter up for annual membership.

BAD-TALKING BOYS

I can't remember how it happened, but somewhere along the way Trevor became that friend in my life whose sole function was to listen to me as I bad-talked boys I was dating. We'd talk for hours on the phone. I'd rant and rave about how disappointed I was in X for doing Y, and Trevor would be all consolation and comfort, saying things like: *You did the right thing by dumping him* or *He's a snake!* or *It's not you it's him* or *Don't worry you'll find him – every bread have its cheese.*

I mean, is it so bad to carry lunch to a guy at work?

This was me one night, telling Trevor about my latest romantic debacle.

It was a thoughtful gesture, he said.

And it was *his* idea! When I cooked dinner for him once he told me, and I quote, *I wish I had someone who would bring me incredible food like this for lunch.*

I guess he wasn't such a fan of your cooking after all, Trevor said, snickering.

Are you saying my cooking is crap? I said.

I'm just saying maybe he was being polite.

Well whatever, I said. I think Fareez overreacted. I mean there were a lot of people in the office – I had no idea that particular dentist's office was so popular, did you? – but to say I somehow embarrassed him by dropping off lunch for him is a bit of a stretch.

Maybe he's really uptight about what people think about him, Trevor said.

It's a shame, I said. He had a huge cock. Did I tell you about his cock?

You did, Trevor said.

For a short little dental assistant, that guy was seriously packing, I said. I think I was just blinded by how hot he was. I mean when he exchanged rings with me, I did think it was a little soon. But he was so cute.

Clearly, he just wanted to get into your pants, Trevor said.

The things a good lolo does to one's brain, I sighed.

I met Trevor one night after I went to Brooklyn Bar.

Notwithstanding its name, Brooklyn Bar was located on a street corner in the heart of Woodbrook. The bar had been around for decades, but its most recent claim to fame was being the setting of a viral video featuring the bar's resident doubles vendor, the son of a government minister, a heated conversation, and an alarmingly large machete. It was a Friday night in August, half past seven. I had taken Mother to the clinic again and after we got home, I needed to blow some steam. In those days, I did this thing where I'd walk down from St James to Brooklyn Bar, then go across to Shakers, then maybe to the Corner Bar or Drink! Wine Bar, before ending the night at Club Studio, next to Invaders pan yard, wining hard on some man to the steelpan music.

Tonight, though, I wasn't sure I had energy for all that. The incident with the machete had done little to stop patrons (if anything more people started coming because they'd forgotten you could drink *and* get doubles and were now reminded of this). There was the usual crowd: the office people who had come straight from work; the gargoyles who sat staring at the large TVs above the bar showing an assortment of sports; the single people on swivel stools who were looking; the couples for whom Brooklyn Bar was part of their "date night" itinerary;

and the fitness fanatics who stopped by after a run or a hike because this was what fitness conscious people in Trinidad liked to do: sweat then drink. Some nights the bar would be filled with buff, half-naked men and women who drove jeeps and trucks and four-wheel drives. Tonight, there was one such group of guys. They wore sweatbands and neon exercise shorts. One of them held an incredibly well-trained Rottweiler on a red leash like an accessory. The dog panted his approval as the men laughed and smiled, holding beers and languidly leaning on their Land Rover parked next to them. I got up to go play with the dog (dogs love me), thinking I would use that as a way in to start chatting up one of the guys, but the dog started to growl and froth and the men looked at me, with my Goth Nevermore t-shirt and baggy trousers, like I was an alien who had just dropped from outer space. I swerved away and walked down the street to Ariapita Avenue for a gyro to call it a night.

Five hours later, I was in Club Studio. I moved among the men like moving through an enchanted forest: some of the guys were tall and thin, others stout and solid, some adorned with foliage, others bare and bark-like. A delicate fog gave everything a soft haze. A mirror ball was like a water-sunk sun that changed and changed and changed its colour as though trying out outfits before going out. The DJ was blasting soca (Patrice Roberts, whom I loved) but then switched to reggae (why? I pondered, why?) so I decided to call it quits. Again. It was after one and I was not in the mood to walk home this late so I phoned a taxi. Trevor came less than a minute later.

That first night, Trevor was wearing a white shirt-jack that gave off serious Hot Daddy vibes even though he was younger than me. His black, pleated trousers were tight on his tree-trunk legs but bunched at his crotch. He was incredibly polite, too polite in fact, and I had to ask him to stop calling me Mr Denny, telling him, repeatedly, to just say Kyle.

I soon started to hire him every time I had to take Mom for dialysis, or every time I needed a lift home from somewhere. I liked the fact that he was handsome. I liked the fact that he was self-employed. I liked that he didn't judge me, that he didn't mind picking me up at 4am outside Club Studio or Euphoria or that place up at St Augustine with the name I could never remember. I liked the fact that he never asked me why I didn't drive (a car accident when I was 11 turned me off driving forever). Meanwhile, he liked the fact that I took care of my mother. He liked the fact that I worked hard at whatever project I was doing (though secretly I knew my job at the Ministry of Community Development, Youth Affairs and the Arts was a shit storm). He liked the fact that I was curious about the world and liked to try new things. He was a taxi driver only for now, he'd say, but he wanted things, wanted a family. Maybe he could join the Defence Force and become a soldier. Or maybe he could become a trainer and have classes in the Savannah like his friend Jameson. Or maybe he could expand his taxi business, branch out and form his own taxi company, with a network of cars and drivers serving different parts of Trinidad and Tobago. Sometimes, when he picked me up, he'd blast Drake in the car and I could tell he was in a wistful mood about something and we'd both talk about the future and what might be and I'd enthuse about my latest dating prospect and he'd say how glad he was that things were looking up. Then, he'd drop me wherever I was going.

Funnily enough, I met my next romantic calamity, Damon, through my job. The Ministry of Community Development, Youth Affairs, and the Arts was located on Frederick Street. The apportioning of departmental office space was in exact correspondence with the ministry's name: Community Development got the lion's share, followed by Youth Affairs, followed by three rooms and a kitchenette for the Arts. I was in the cubicle that oversaw policy formulation, though sometimes I was also put in charge of random cultural projects like hosting touring Chinese drummers or organising micro music festivals in the countryside featuring imported yogis, local hippies and vegan food vendors. I knew there was no real future for me in the post of "Policy Officer". I was on contract, which was another way of saying I was fucked, and it was clear to me that nobody seriously cared about "the Arts" beyond, perhaps, the entertainment segment that you sometimes have at swanky government events – you know, the part of the event where the Shiv Shakti dancers come on to entertain the crowd or the Laventille Rhythm Section or maybe Neval Chatelal, a few steelpan players and some jacked up Moko Jumbies. I secretly wanted to be something else, anything else. Maybe a counsellor. I was a good listener. Or at least that's what I had heard from Trevor who had started to call me to complain about his girlfriend. I thought perhaps I could try and get into some kind of psychology programme abroad. But that was a lot of money, even if I could put together some funding. No, I stayed in the job because the hours were relatively flexible, which was important because that allowed me to take Mom to her appointments.

One day, I was at my desk when the phone rang. I dreaded answering my hotline because sometimes I got crackpots who just wanted to call and speechify about how retrograde the country's culture policy was, or some such stuff way over my pay grade.

Is this Kyle Denny? the person on the other end said.

The one and only, I replied.

Hi, I got your name from the operator, he said. I was calling to ask whether there are any special grants for musicians to record albums.

Damon was a gospel singer who wanted to record his latest album *See You When I Return Back*. There were no grants as far as I was aware but I told him that supporting upcoming musicians was important to the ministry and I would get back to him shortly. I found him online. His Instagram was filled with videos of him playing a guitar and singing. He had a honeyed voice, and a gorgeous collection of fashionably tattered sweaters that he always wore in his videos. And he had the greatest thunder thighs since Hasely Crawford at the 1976 Montreal Olympics.

We started exchanging messages, and soon Damon was coming over to my place. He said he was recording the album in Woodbrook and would come over in between recording sessions because he needed inspiration. In addition to his legs, I was turned on by the fact that he was a musician – which was a first for me – and also by his voice (he would sing in the shower after sex). Yes, he really was into Jesus and all that, but I didn't think I should hold it against him. I was a lapsed Catholic and I understood how much faith could mean to someone. On my sofa we would have long, tearful conversations about the idea of angels watching over us, about our lives having some hidden pattern or destiny. One day he brought his guitar and we wrote a song together, which he posted on Instagram. He called it 'The String', in a reference to the idea of an invisible thread tying people meant to be in love together.

The problems started when I suggested we go out for a drink. Damon always met me at my place (in the evenings when Mother was asleep in her part of the house) because he said it was near to where he was recording the album in Woodbrook. His apartment was out of bounds, he said, because he had nosy neighbours who would see me, which would be bad because he didn't want them to think he was gay or anything. This was his first time with a guy, he said, tearfully, a cliché which I knew very likely was untrue, but went along with anyhow because, well, thunder thighs, and it was easier to believe in him than to face reality.

He's on the down low, Trevor said after I discussed Damian with him when the affair ended. He's just one of those.

I know a few, I said demurely. But still, this guy was depressing. I mean I thought I could deal with the whole Vampire-Never-Be-In-The-Daylight thing, but man. A guy just needs to wine on his bae now and then in a fete, sheesh.

How did it end? Trevor asked.

Would you imagine? He started chatting up one of my friends. I mean, how sleazy is that? All that bullshit about fate and destiny and muses and Jesus and he was just looking to get laid.

Nothing wrong with just wanting to get laid, Trevor pointed out.

Yes, I know, but all the pretence and hypocrisy. He's this gospel singer singing all these virtuous songs about the truth and can't even face up to himself.

Listen, he's just not at that stage. Don't take it personally, Trevor said.

It makes me mad, I said. But damn, that Jesus sex was good.

The Trevor sex started the night I talked to him about dumping Claude because I realised what a jackass Claude was.

I'd met Claude on OkCupid. He was an actor with a local theatre troupe called The Roving Players and every time we met he would enthuse about how great the director of the company, Arthur Napoleon, was. Acting meant everything to Claude. It gave him freedom. He could shed his self like a skin and become someone different on the stage for a few hours. He could learn things, steep himself in new skills, satisfy his curiosity for life. He had studied the teachings of Konstantin

Stanislavski, Jacques Lecoq, and Denis Diderot. His favourite
actors were Nicole Kidman and Daniel Day-Lewis. He loved
the theatre. We went to the Little Carib Theatre and saw *Moon
Over a Rainbow Shawl*, *Miss Miles*, and an impressive staging of
Equus featuring sexy male Carnival dancers as the horses. I was
drawn to how passionate Claude was, more so given the fact
that acting had played a key role during a particularly a difficult
time in his life. He'd had cancer and undergone chemotherapy.
But he had survived, in part because of his love of the stage.
Acting, he said one night as he held my hands, had saved his life.

Things changed when I went to see him act. The play was
called *Jestina Finds A Husband*. Arthur Napoleon was known
for staging classic comedies like *Calabash Lane*. Claude played
a potential suitor for Jestina. He delivered his lines in a
booming, stilted manner, which jarred me a bit because his
grasp of craft had seemed so sophisticated from all that he had
told me. But I didn't think he was *that* bad. He was simply
matching the tone of the piece, following the director's
vision. In fact, I was relieved to find that he had a sense of
humour and that the play was even funnier because of how
overdone the acting was. I was there with Claude's mother
and we sat in the front row. Meryl clapped her son fiercely
and gave him a standing ovation every time he had a scene.
During the intermission, I chatted with her and told her how
wonderful it was that acting had become Claude's calling
after it had helped him survive cancer.

What cancer? she asked, perplexed.

Didn't Claude have cancer? I said, almost spilling my plastic
cup of wine.

Where on earth would you get such an idea? she said. Claude
doesn't have an unhealthy bone in his body.

After the play, I went backstage to speak with Claude. When
I got to the dressing room, I found him with Arthur Napoleon.

They were making out and didn't notice when I appeared in the tiny room with white walls.

That's rough, Trevor said. He was a good actor after all.

I guess, I said.

Anyhow, can I come over tonight? Trevor said. We can watch a movie, though I guess you don't want to see any actors right now.

A few hours later, Trevor was in my room. Mom was already asleep. We chatted for a bit over some beers. Then, he connected his phone to my Bluetooth and started playing Drake.

What are you doing? I said.

Playing music, he said. I always play music when I have sex.

We're going to have sex? I said.

He came over and kissed me. He didn't taste like how I imagined he might taste. He didn't smell like how I had imagined he might smell. He was brand-new, his tongue, his fingers in my hair, the way he pressed me closer to him.

I think I may need some time to process all this, I said, gasping for breath.

What was it Aristotle said? Trevor declared. *The best way to get over one man is to get under another?*

I don't think he quite said that, I said, but he should have.

Trevor undressed, neatly folding his clothes and placing them on the bureau by the door. We sometimes went to the beach and had seen each other naked before. But seeing him in this new light felt different, even if the essence of him was unchanged, like a house you've been to before that's been newly renovated. He took off my t-shirt. He took off my trousers. He took off his watch and put it on the bureau too, but he kept on his thick gold chain with the Ankh pendant he wore. It felt hard and pleasing against my flesh as he leaned in and kissed me again. Drake got louder and louder, his voice abrasive yet supple. Out of the speaker, dulcet missiles spurted:

Tell me who the fuck you wanna be
Before I turn the lights out

I hadn't been a fan of Drake before. But eventually, because Trevor liked to play Drake every time we had sex, I soon knew entire Drake songs by heart.

After that first night, Trevor kept coming over to my place, kept driving Mom and me to her dialysis appointments, and telling me about all the crazy customers that filled his day. Sometimes, after sex he'd get into these moods because he felt guilty about cheating on his girlfriend Olga, who was really a nice person. He'd say he was going to tell her. But we both knew he was just performing. He was never going to tell his girlfriend. He was never going to tell anyone. This was just a small thing, no big deal. He was straight. And I was busy with my job and with taking care of Mother and with all my attempts at finding love. It was just friendly sex. You know, the sex you have to get through a rough patch or to take up the time. And I was cool with that because I knew Trevor was as unavailable to me as I was to him. Therefore, we could safely be available to each other every now and then.

The next guy was yet another musician, which confirmed my soft spot for guys who played instruments.

Stalin – he was named after a local calypsonian, not the Russian dictator – played the piano. I started chatting with him on Messenger after he posted a video of himself playing Liszt.

He was really, really into his music, I said to Trevor one afternoon when he'd come over again. Drake was oozing out of the speakers:

These girls ain't got nothing on you
They ain't got nothing on you

His name alone tells me where this one's going, Trevor said.

Stalin lived down south with his mother. He'd gone to Julliard in the States and was a concert pianist (though nobody I knew had ever heard of him). We'd have these long conversations about his favourite composers. His favourite was Schumann (on the strength of the *Ghost Variations*). He was obsessed with how he looked, updating his Facebook profile image almost daily. He wore lots of beaded jewellery. Whenever we spoke (our entire interaction was online) he'd end the conversation by sending a recording of himself playing the piano, choosing some piece that he felt was relevant to the conversation. One night, after two weeks of chatting, he told me how wonderful I was and how glad he was that I was in his life and that he loved me.

Another Fareez? Trevor said, laughing. You exchanged rings too?

I was shocked, I said. But you know what happens to me in these moments. My brain tells me *run* but my dick says something else entirely. I mean I'd never even actually met this guy in person and yet here I was writing back *I love you too.*

Things started to go downhill with Stalin when he told me the story of how he became a pianist. His father had wanted to be a pianist all his life but never became one. But Stalin was good at the piano and became the pianist his father had dreamed of being. He told me everything he did, all the classes he took, all the practice, all the research and training – he did it for his father.

And then his father died, I told Trevor.

Noooo, said Trevor, sitting up. That must have been rough for him.

It was. He went through an existential crisis. Who am I? What am I? What should I be doing with my life? He told me that he stopped doing recitals and concerts in order to grieve for his father because he knew going on without him would not feel the same. At the same time, he said he loved the piano and would always love it. I asked him whether he loved the piano because he had used it to please his father. He rejected the idea as foolish.

I mean, some people don't like it when you offer them your outsider's perspective, Trevor said.

Then, one day I notice he's all terse and quiet in his messages. Which was odd because saying *hello* to him would normally result in a full Independence Day presidential address. I asked him if he was okay and he said *yes*. Then I asked if he was upset and he said *no*. He kept giving me short, uninterested replies. So I told him it was cool knowing him. Then, I get a message saying: *Ask Stalin why he leaves his phone unlocked. This is his mother, Barbarella. I've been monitoring your messages to my son. It's not your business to tell him not to play the piano anymore.*

What the hell! Trevor said.

Exactly my sentiment, I said, taking off my Marilyn Manson t-shirt and getting into position to suck Trevor off. It was way, way too much bacchanal for me.

One night, after Trevor finished in me, we were in the backseat of his car, which was parked at the beach. He'd picked me up for a late afternoon swim and we'd grabbed some beers and driven to Tyrico Bay, had a dip, then hung out on the beach as the sun set over the languid waves. The car smelled of cum, sea salt and forest. I told him about Poormar, a guy I'd started dating over Christmas.

I almost don't want to tell even you the sordid details, I said.

But then I did exactly that, relating a long and involved narrative in which I had gone all out for yet another guy who turned out to be a fuckboy. For Poormar I had, at one point, gone into the countryside and picked wildflowers, braving razor grass and insects, in order to present him with a bouquet of flowers when he was sick. When I turned up to his house in Maracas St Joseph to surprise him with the flowers, he was with another man.

Who picks wildflowers for people? Trevor laughed.

Clearly, I do, I said.

Trevor held me in his arms. The sea breeze had become chilly and he was nice and warm.

I didn't tell Olga, but I'm going too soon, he said. It just wasn't the right moment.

I want to cum again, I said, shutting him up with a kiss.

When I got home that night, Mom was in my room. She had on the light blue duster I'd gotten her for Christmas, which gave her a ghostly, yet strangely chic Boho appearance.

Where have you been? she asked, though she already knew the answer.

At the beach, I said, with Trevor.

You've been seeing a lot of him lately, she said, smiling.

Not really, I said. I'd say maybe every now and then we see each other.

Kyle, I may be a sick woman but my ears still work. I hear what goes on here at night, even though you play that dumb rap music to try to cover your tracks. Are you two a couple now? He's such an attractive gentleman. A *real* gentleman.

Eww mom, please, I said. And no, we're not a couple. We're just friends.

Why? she said. I don't get your generation you know. You'd be wonderful together. You have such a great rapport.

And obviously you enjoy spending lots of quality time with him.

He doesn't identify as queer. He identifies as straight. He has a girlfriend.

So then why are you wasting your time with him?

We're friends. We enjoy each other's company and that's that. That's enough for us.

Is it? she said.

Mom, things today don't work like they used to, you know. This whole idea that you're supposed to find The One and settle down forever, that Mr Darcy or Mr Rochester is going to come riding on horseback and sweep you off to Pemberley Park or Thornfield Hall – people don't buy that crap anymore. Relationships work differently now. In fact, they've always worked in varied, non-hegemonic ways.

But don't you have dreams for yourself? What about a family? What about the counselling you wanted to do? Don't you think it might be good to go away? Maybe you could find somebody there?

I can study here, I said. And I can find somebody here too.

Okay, okay, she said. But remember, life's short. Take it from me. And I'm not going to be alive forever you know. Soon, I'll be gone and you'll have no more excuses for wasting the best years of your life.

Mom, I'm not wasting my life, I said. I'm living it.

Sure, she said. Anyhow, can you tell me where the red pills are, I looked all over when you were out and couldn't find them.

They're on the top shelf next to the erythropoietin, I said.

Later, in bed, with the smell of Trevor and the sea still on me, I thought about whether Mother had a point. I mean the Ministry was bad. Really bad. And it didn't matter which government was in power. They all came into office with Big

Talk and then boiled down like bhaji. After five to ten years somebody else comes in and the cycle starts over.

The counselling thing – could I really find a way?

Could I make it happen, with my pay?

And Trevor and me?

A couple?

A thing? I mean it wouldn't be *that* bad.

But it wasn't entirely up to me, was it? It wasn't like Trevor was available to me in the way I needed him to be. Maybe life could simply continue this way. And maybe that was okay. Besides, who would I bad-talk boys with if Trevor and I ever starting dating?

BELMONT

We always knew Father would leave. We just didn't know when.

On Saturday mornings he would wake us by putting on his favourite record: *Vladimir Horowitz Plays Beethoven*. When we came out in our pajamas, the curtains of the living room would be drawn. Father would be blasting the "Emperor Concerto", which seemed an odd name for something so twinkly. In the armchair he had built himself, his leg would dangle over the armrest as he conducted the music, drank coffee, and read from *The Sentinel*, his favourite newspaper. Each sleepy child would be directed to the kitchen, not for breakfast but to read the roster of weekend chores he had carefully drafted and left on the fridge. If any child complained, Father would read out some article from his newspaper about global suffering.

You're lucky you're not a child growing up in Azerbaijan right now, he'd say. Or: Things are pretty bad in Haiti these days.

This Saturday morning routine started after we moved to Belmont. For years, we had lived in a cramped, cockroach-infested apartment on George Street in downtown Port of Spain. When my brother Jean-Paul was born, Father said we needed more room. For what seemed like a long time, Father would be away on weekends, coming back to George Street on Sunday evenings wearing tattered clothes speckled with paint, as though he were an artist. He would smell of sweat and sawdust, a mixture I would forever associate with him.

One night in the apartment on George Street, Father came into our bedroom. Sahara and Libya were asleep. But I was still awake, secretly reading a novel I had borrowed from the library.

Time to go, he said.

Time to go where? I asked.

Yeah, where? Sahara said, groggily.

Your mother waiting outside, he said.

Sahara was the oldest girl. It was her job to marshal the troops.

Usha, put that book away and let's go! she told me.

When we got outside, Mother was already in the truck. She was wearing a bandana over her thinning hair and had a basket of freshly baked bread. The back of the truck held mysterious boxes and was covered with blue tarpaulin. Mother held Jean-Paul, and I sat on Sahara's lap. Father put Libya in the back, because she was always tomboyish.

We drove to the outskirts of the city. There was a full moon, but I did not know where we were going. The big buildings of the city gave way to strange gingerbread houses, tightly packed roads, narrow lanes. Then the truck veered sharply up a hill. It struggled to kick into gear and Father made an impassioned plea.

C'mon Betsy!

We made it to a white house at the top of the hill that overlooked the city. I remember being frightened to climb out of the truck, because the sparkling lights below us filled me with a sense of danger. This was a place where you could easily fall.

The house was sparse. The bare concrete floors were rough and cool. On that first night we slept on a mattress in one of the empty bedrooms. Father later built two sets of double-deckers, and got second-hand rugs with pictures of elephants and the Taj Mahal.

In those days, Father and Mother rarely quarrelled. Their joy at finally having a boy child was palpable. They had been trying for years. I was nine, Sahara thirteen and Libya seven. Almost when they'd given up, Jean-Paul arrived.

We grew accustomed to our new life in Belmont. Mother asked Father to make a boxed garden. She planted tomatoes and I planted a tamarind seed. On mornings, Mother would make warm chocolate milk to go with breakfast. Father would drive me to school in his taxi. He liked to avoid the rush-hour traffic by taking exciting shortcuts. Once, we drove along the entire length of the St Francois Valley Road, passing commuters standing patiently waiting for cars, students buying doubles for breakfast, and parents holding hands with their children. The morning sunlight turning them all into shadows.

★

Things changed the year my parents got married. The day it happened, they came back from church and cut a cake. Father told us he wanted to get married because that was one of the sacraments and Granny would have wanted him to do it. I had seen movies and watched Princes Diana marry Prince Charles and had the impression weddings were grand things. When Mother came back from church wearing a simple white blouse and a skirt I thought it strange. The only hint of festivity was her floral bangle.

It was when Father brought Frances to live with us that the quarrelling started.

Frances was a student who went to school with me at Belmont Girls RC. We used to talk to each other a lot at recess and one day we both discovered something that changed everything.

My mum says you are my sister and your dad is my dad, Frances said.

Who is your mother? I said.

She used to work the same place as your dad, but she going back Grenada.

When I got home I asked Mother if this was true. Mother said nothing and continued peeling potatoes. Then she told me to do my homework.

There was a huge fight that night.

Don't let me find where I put my belt, Father said one time.

Bring it nah, Mother replied. You jackass.

You-you-you see you? Father stuttered when he got angry. He picked up a potted plant from the hall, holding it like a weapon.

Leave my kissmeass plant alone! Mother said. You feel you buy that or what?

I'd never heard them quarrel like this before.

That weekend, Father went out and when he came back Frances was with him.

Sahara took off her Walkman, looked Frances up and down, and said, I'm going into my room. Father frowned. Mother asked Frances if she would like something to eat. The girl seemed confused.

The first night, Frances slept in my room. By this stage, the house had changed. We each had bedrooms of our own and Father had abandoned his idea of having a house with no doors. (I don't like doors, he used to say.)

Libya and I helped Father paint the spare bedroom. We put in a desk and a bookshelf. This became Frances's room. Whenever she was not around, I would sneak and look at what books she was reading. At nights, I would hear whenever she switched off her lamp just before bed.

Father would drop us all to school. The car would be silent.

In school, Frances and I stopped talking. She started liming with older girls. She would walk home with them, following them as they explored Belmont's labyrinth of lanes. She said she found a shortcut to our home but never showed me.

One day, Mother cooked lentils, a meal Frances didn't like. The girl looked at the food in disgust when Mother set the plate before her, then asked if she could have something else. Mother told her if she didn't like her cooking she could go live elsewhere. Frances cried. When Father came home that night, Frances was still at the table, the soggy grey stuff in front of her.

We started having Prayer Night.

The family that prays together stays together, Father would say. He would marshal everyone. He read random passages from the Bible (he believed in plucking them out through a process of divine accident) and we would have to say an entire rosary, with each person given the task of mouthing invocations that seemed to last decades.

As the weeks went by, Prayer Night grew more elaborate. Before each session, Father would fill a thurible with incense and fumigate the house. (I had no idea where he got the thurible from, but later it emerged he was very friendly with the church ladies.)

Dad, are you trying to bless us or kill us? Sahara asked him one day through the thick smoke. He simply walked up to her and sprinkled holy water over her, whispering something. He got his holy water from the abbey at Mount St Benedict; it was kept it in a bottle that grew cloudy as the weeks went by. I thought of the amoebas growing in the water whenever he sprinkled the cold droplets on us as we prayed.

One day in December, five months after moving in, Frances did not come home from school. Mother stood with her arms folded in the yard, looking over the wrought-iron gate. When he came home from evening mass, he went out in the streets to look for Frances. Nothing.

That night Father convened an emergency Prayer Night and prayed intently for Frances's safety. I did too. I had already decided I was agnostic and normally wouldn't get worked up by all the invocations, but that night a part of me wanted to believe praying would make a difference.

The next morning Father got a call from a woman. He told us Frances was with her mother in Gonzales, the town adjoining Belmont, and would come back soon.

Frances never came back.

★

Though the quarrelling died down, things never settled after that.

On Saturdays, instead of playing his Beethoven record, Father would play Handel's *Messiah*. Jean-Paul would spend his time skulking around the house and Mother would sometimes find him and give him a haircut as my sisters watched TV. I'd go outside to tend the plants; my once-delicate tamarind tree had grown so large the box garden began to bulge and crack.

It wasn't long before Father started talking in his sleep. Sahara and I would creep up to our parents' bedroom and listen.

Play it again Sam, he'd say, as though chatting affectionately with a friend. But then he would cry out, What are you doing to me? He would toss and turn and we would become worried he might wake. Mother never woke. She could sleep through anything. In the mornings, when Father sang in the shower, I would marvel at how polished his voice sounded compared with the fragile voice he used when dreaming.

I was now going to secondary school at Holy Name Convent, Father would pick me up every day, even though it was close to Belmont and I could comfortably walk. He wasn't taking any chances, he said, especially after what had happened to Mrs. Lockwood's daughter Anastasia. Everyone in church had heard about the incident when a man held Anastasia at knifepoint and robbed her on Archer Street.

Father became a reader at church. It was something he took as seriously as Prayer Night. Before mass, he'd practice reading out the short passages from the Bible. Whenever he made a mistake, Mrs. Lockwood would tell him about it and he would agonise over his marred oratory when he got home.

Eventually, Father roped Jean-Paul into the readers' circle. Jean-Paul had tried, unsuccessfully, to become an altar boy. He was dropped from acolyte class after it was discovered he was interested in the job only because of the flowing robes he would get to wear.

Father never tried to get me involved in church. He said I was very bright and had to focus on beating my books because I was studying for my O Level examinations. Sahara certainly had enough on her plate at university. Libya was too busy focusing on trying to enter teen pageants and becoming a model.

I was thinking about this the day Father was late picking me up. He was never late. Maybe a passenger had asked for a drop somewhere off-route. I chatted with the snow cone man in the park across the street and waited.

When Father's white Nissan Datsun drove up, the man inside the car seemed like another person. He opened the door for me, with a relaxed smile. It was only when I buckled myself in that I realised there was someone else.

Usha, this is Evelyn. Evelyn, this is Usha. I shook hands awkwardly with the mother of Frances.

We went for a drive around the Savannah. Then we walked

through the Botanical Gardens. Evelyn held my hand as we walked, holding me tighter than she should, as though she was nervous of losing property belonging to someone else. She told me Frances was now living in Grenada with her grandmother and bought me an ice-cream cone that melted faster than I could eat it.

When I got home, I felt I had betrayed Mother. I said nothing and slammed the door to my bedroom, my hands cold and sticky.

★

That Saturday, when we woke there was no music. In the living room where Father would normally be, there was no one. The sateen satchel he had made to carry his Bible, rosary and holy water was gone.

Nobody said anything.

Mother spent most of the day acting as if nothing was wrong, nobody was missing. Sahara confronted her.

This is bullshit! Are you guys getting divorced or something? Why the hell did you get married in the first place?

Mother put the kettle to boil.

★

When my examination results came out weeks later and the school informed us that I had done very well, Father still had not come back. We had a good notion where he was, but the idea of it was unmentionable.

But I knew Mother was thinking about him. One day, she devised a plan. She told me to put on my school uniform. She arranged an interview with a newspaper. The next day a big story about my examination success appeared on the front page, complete with a photo of Mother and me.

BELMONT SCHOLAR
By Imogen Fletcher, Friday, July 7, 1999

THE BELEAGUERED people of that nefarious hotspot known as Belmont – whose community has long fallen prey to rampant crime, poverty and dire hopelessness – today can feel justifiably proud after one of their own, Usha Maraj, broke through all of their adversity to achieve excellence in the Caribbean Examination Council O Level examination and earn top place in the country.

"It is not a question of where one lives, but a question of one's mentality," the 16-year-old scholar told *The Sentinel* yesterday after she and her proud single-parent mother, Agnes Maraj-Huggins, visited this newspaper's St Vincent Street, Port-of-Spain head-office to share the good news. Maraj hopes her success will inspire others in her community and other economically-depressed areas around the country, to strive for excellence, no matter what their circumstances may be or whence they originate.

Asked if she felt her top score was a sign that where you are from does not determine whether you can make it, young, soft-spoken Maraj said she never thought of Belmont as anything but home. "Home is home and where you live shouldn't really matter. Once your work ethic is good, once you have ambition that's what counts."

Maraj studied Pure Maths, Applied Maths, Physics and Chemistry, among the brainiest subjects a student can pursue. She said she wanted to study English Literature and described reading the Brontë sisters (the famous family comprising of Emily, Jane, and Anne) as one of her favourite hobbies, but in the end felt she

needed to do science subjects. Her wise decision paid
off. She attained full distinctions. The fact that she has
earned top place in the country was still something that
shocked her. "It feels surreal. But all the same, it's a
nice, wonderful feeling."

As she spoke to *The Sentinel*, Maraj's single-parent
mother, Agnes Maraj-Huggins, could not help but
smile as it was clear she was proud of her daughter. She
said she was not surprised by her family's success and
stressed the importance of the role of a parent or parents
in charting the course of their children's lives.

Mother cut out this article and had it framed. She hung it in
the living room, where Father's crucifix used to be. We got lots
of phone calls and the house became busy. Family members
whom we had not heard from in decades came back.

★

Not long after the story appeared, Father drove up outside the
house. I thought I saw Mother smile, but so briefly I wondered
if I had seen it at all. Father gave me some pink flowers and a
box of chocolate and said he was proud of me. He was still
sitting in the kitchen when Sahara came home.

What you doing here? You only come back because of her?
she said. Like you only have one daughter or what?

Sahara, don't be like that, Father said. This is an important
achievement for Usha.

For you you mean! Sahara said. She stormed off to call her
university boyfriend, Baldwin. I always thought his round face
looked a lot like Father's.

Father didn't stick around after that to see Jean-Paul or
Libya. He got up, told Mother goodbye and made his way to the
door. The words jumped out of me.

Daddy, I love you. Don't go, I said.

I'll come back, Father said.

I watched him drive off in the white car. I stood in our yard and remembered that night when we first made it to the top of the hill, seeing the lights of houses below, hundreds of lights sparkling like a Christmas tree and I was frightened because suddenly you could fall.

THE FOREST RANGER

1.

They drove along Edwards Trace, the lonely trail that cut across the Victoria-Mayaro Forest Reserve. The road was bad. At one point, it crossed a steep ravine but the wooden bridge was so rotten it was possible the 4x4 was too heavy and would fall through. Felix was intent on following the tip, so he drove on. But Aloes, who would normally be eager for an adventure in the bush, told him to stop the truck. He got out.

I not dying on this secret mission, I telling you now, Aloes said. He walked across the rickety bridge and waited with his arms folded, his shoulders broad.

Felix adjusted the gears and it was as though the truck took a deep breath before lurching forward. The wooden beams of the bridge looked like a giant xylophone as the truck crossed, its tyres making weird musical noises. Once over, Felix stopped. Aloes jumped in like a bodyguard rejoining a convoy.

In the distance, the Trinity Hills rose, three stone faces peeking out from under a green duvet of canopies. They arrived at the giant Mora tree, the one everyone, including illegal hunters, used as a landmark to indicate they had reached the centre of the reserve. It was one of Felix's favourite trees in the reserve (perhaps his second favourite – his favourite was another tree at the secret spot he often visited far away from here). Its leaves were pinkish brown. Its heavy beans hung like long, rusty machetes. All around, young Mora seedlings and saplings formed a dense, scarcely penetrable growth, turning this part of the forest floor into a miniature forest with its own canopy. Felix consulted the map he had sketched when he got the call. He looked around but couldn't see anything unusual. The trunk of the giant Mora tree was adorned with elkhorn ferns, Carnival headpieces pointing up, up, up into the sky. Felix had a strong sense that this forest was not simply a collection of trees, but rather a single organism telling him something. It was what he liked about his job. Except on days like today.

Aloes saw it first. In the middle of the thick forest, a sudden clearing, as though a giant hand had flattened everything with a lawn roller. It was a wide avenue, the width of ten car lanes. At its centre was a yellow pipeline buttressed above the ground with hundreds of small crutches. Its very straightness made it look unnatural.

Felix had been sceptical about the tip. How could such a thing happen without anybody knowing or saying anything until now? But now he knew for sure.

2.

When they got back, the Forestry Division in Pleasantville was almost deserted. It was a small, one-storey building with a reception desk and a cashier's booth to the front. Mr Orville, the Acting Conservator of Forests, was still there, busily affixing signs on a notice board for the next day. One read:

Hunters please note that an amendment was made to the caged bird permit and as such you are only allowed to catch cravat, parakeet and semp birds. An amend-

ment was also made to the waterfowl permit. Please
check the back of the permit for further information.

Mr Orville was always annoyed when the laws were tinkered
with because it meant putting up new signs. He said: Why
don't these parliamentarians just fix all the laws once and for all
and let us get on with our work? He pressed hard on a
thumbtack as though he was enforcing the law itself.

For all his bravado, Felix wasn't in the habit of addressing
Mr Orville directly. But now he spoke up.

Leviathan Corp is running a gas line right through the centre
of the reserve, he said.

Mr Orville stopped what he was doing, looked around as
though checking to see if anyone else was around, then told
Felix and Aloes to follow him into his office.

The Government made them sign an agreement, Mr Orville
said as he shut the door. They not supposed to touch the
reserve. You sure?

I got a tip they were clearing land, Felix said. We just got
back. It was bad. The pipeline is practically done. They've cut
down thousands of trees already.

Aloes showed Mr Orville photos on his phone. Mr Orville
looked at the images. Tears came to his eyes.

Look at how much they've cleared, he said, his voice break-
ing as he spoke. I'll have to take this up with the Ministry
immediately. Have you sent these to anyone else?

They shook their heads.

Mr Orville got up and held the door open for them to leave
his office.

Send the images to me. I'll need them tonight, he said. As he
closed the door, he paused to say: Good job fellas.

3.

As usual they were in the rum shop around the corner, but instead of spending hours complaining about how meaningless it was to have just two forest rangers to protect hundreds and hundreds of acres of forest, they had cause to celebrate. As they sat on the benches outside, looking at traffic drive by, they knew what they didn't need to say: that their discovery was the first time they'd done anything in all the years they'd been working together that meant remotely anything. But that discovery was, though, a sign of all they had so far failed to prevent. The pipeline was already up. So many precious trees had already been lost.

I'm getting another Stag, Aloes said, after he emptied his sixth. You want a next one?

Felix knew what the look on Aloes' face was really asking. It was the look that came over him whenever they both got sufficiently drunk, when what had once passed between them briefly flickered.

No, I'm fine. I have to go home to Jasmine, Felix said. Immediately he regretted the reply. He could see that his words were like the cut of a blade that made Aloes wince.

Suit yourself partner, Aloes said. He went up to the bar and started flirting with Daisy, the bartender.

Felix watched as the usual dance played out – Aloes leaning suavely against the counter, his long body relaxed, his legs crossed at the ankles so that his calves bulged beneath his three-quarter khaki trousers, the gold chain around his neck glimmering in the dim light like his toothy smile, talking, talking, spouting a whole set of lyrics that amounted to one simple message: he could satisfy any woman in bed.

Something rose in Felix that he, too, needed to quench. He got up and drove home to Jasmine's harbouring arms.

4.

The Forestry Division in Pleasantville was not far from his home at Moruga. But Felix had got into the habit of making long detours along the way to work, often phoning Aloes to say he was out tagging a tree for inventory or checking a tip about illegal hunting in the off-season. On this morning, he rang Aloes but got no answer so left a message. Then he drove to Basseterre and made the turn to Edwards Trace. He monitored work on the pipeline. It was getting even longer. He continued along the road until he got to the spot where his special trail was. He stopped the car, got out and walked.

The kapok tree was one of the largest on the island. Its huge roots could conceal several men in its folds. Vines festooned its trunk as it pushed to the sky. Near this tree, but deeper into the shade, the vegetation took on a different character. Rare shoe-maker butterflies, which sometimes camouflaged themselves into the ground by closing their wings, sucked on the vegetation's saps and sugars. At this hidden part of the forest reserve there were strange black puddles on the surface of the land, puddles with iridescent skins. Similar skins swirled on the surface of a nearby stream. The land oozed oil.

Felix took out his mobile phone and looked at his recent photos of the giant yellow pipeline that seemed to augur the end of it all: the reserve, his job, his purpose. He'd been thinking of sending the photos to the Environmental Management Authority. They would surely act. He'd grown to doubt Mr Orville. It had been weeks since they told him everything and there was no word on any follow-up. But every time Felix's doubt was on the verge of hardening into all-out distrust, something held him back. Some fear of consequences and implications. He put his phone away and headed back.

5.

When Felix got to the office Aloes was not there. There was a
note on his desk from Mr Orville:
    See me at once.
    I have to compliment you, Mr Orville said as soon as Felix
entered the cramped room. There was a large, frayed map of
the island's forest reserves on the wall. Mr Orville continued:
    Your vigilance and persistence have not gone unnoticed.
You've been summoned to the Ministry in Port of Spain. You
have a meeting with Minister Lashley himself. Take the day off
tomorrow and go.

6.

This high up, you could see the Gulf of Paria stretching into the
distance, its silver-leaf surface sparkling. The skyscraper hous-
ing the headquarters of the Ministry of the Environment was
a brand-new glass and steel tower, which, as a cost-cutting
measure, also housed the headquarters of the Ministry of
Energy a few floors up.
    I've got to go home now, the Minister's private secretary
said. But I'm assured the minister will see you when his
meeting is over. They started a little later than planned.
    She was a short woman who wore her glasses halfway down
her nose so that you thought they might fall off but, miracu-
lously, they never did. She had a red jacket over her shoulders
to stay warm in the cold of the air-conditioned building. She
brought over a small, white Styrofoam plate with a slice of
sweetbread, a cheese-paste sandwich, a chicken puff and a mini
chicken roti, and placed it on the coffee table in front of Felix.
From another meeting today, she said, smiling the way a

mother looks at a son. There was something about the way Felix looked that made people treat him kindly.

Felix sat alone in the empty waiting room. He was wearing the baggy blue suit Jasmine had insisted he wear.

These kinds of people prefer it when you wear suits, Jasmine had said, before adding: You know they say he's going to be prime minister one day. He wants badly to turn the economy around.

In the hour or so of waiting, Felix tried to imagine what having a conversation with the minister would be like. Mr Lashley had a reputation for eloquent parliamentary speeches. Though he was a passionate advocate for environmental causes, he was also known for being careful, meticulous and strategic. It probably took this long for the matter to reach his desk because it had to go through the proper channels. Felix knew he was bad at making small talk with powerful people, so he prepared some mental notes that might serve him in this situation – some mention about being married to his wife for seven years; his hopes that one day his son, Max, would also become a forest ranger. He would mention how there were not enough forest rangers because the pay was simply not good enough (or maybe he should avoid this point because he didn't want to seem cravatious). If the Minister paid him any compliments, he'd turn them around and refer to the Minister's own sterling reputation for green causes and thank him again for the chance to report first-hand what had been going on in the Mayaro Reserve.

The door to the minister's office burst open. A loud gaggle of men in dark, finely-tailored suits spilled out, laughing and making old talk. Felix recognised some from the papers, but most he didn't. When they all left, Mr Lashley emerged. He beckoned Felix to come into the office.

Felix stood in the centre of the room, a deferential smile in place. A huge window gave an unimpeded view of the sea outside – a canvas mottled with barges, ferries, water taxis, small boats, and grey, mysterious blotches, perhaps fuel, perhaps sargassum, perhaps floating islands of rubbish. In front of this glass pane, Mr Lashley sat at a big desk studying some papers. He was sullen. He remained behind the desk and stared at Felix. Then he rose to his feet and came round from behind the desk with remarkable agility. He had a head of grey hair and a thick, solid body. He delivered a resounding slap to the right side of Felix's face.

Don't mess with my business, he said.

Felix had no recollection of leaving the office, travelling down the elevator, and walking through the building's large glass and steel lobby into the ramshackle streets of downtown Port of Spain. Somehow he made it to the car park, then drove past the Brian Lara Promenade where men sat playing chess and vagrants slept on cardboard boxes.

7.

When he got home, Jasmine had a worried look on her face.

Did you hear? she said.

What? Felix said.

Aloes was in a car accident. He's dead.

8.

Early the next morning, Felix got the call from Mr Orville.

Look here, I'm sorry but you have been let go. Don't bother to pick up your things, we'll send them with a driver. The Public Service Commission will be in contact soon to settle terms.

9.

Some weeks after Aloes' funeral, the locusts came. Neighbours saw them in the distance and called out to Felix and his family. Everyone went outside and looked. Over the serrated edge of the hills in the distance, a streak of rust-coloured air.

Felix told his wife and son to go back inside. He shut the front door. The air darkened. It was a strange kind of darkness. The sky became a grainy film, a canvas of jumping, jerking pockmarks and particles. There were thuds and bangs of locusts falling onto roofs or slamming against walls, windows, doors. Soon they covered the front yard.

Felix waited for the swarm to die down and went back inside.

Not many people had come to Aloes' funeral. He was single, didn't have children, had few connections. At the small church, called La Divina Pastora, Felix had gazed up at the stained-glass window with a scene of Jesus preaching to a crowd with green rolling hills in the distance. The hills were meant to be the Trinity Hills, but they didn't look like them. Felix looked at his friend, his partner, lying there in the cheap, unlined casket, his smooth, symmetrical face oddly mis-shapen as though in mid-thought when death interrupted. His thick, beautiful lips were thicker now, yet more firmly shut. Felix allowed himself to remember what happened that night years ago at Aloes' house, something that had never happened before (he didn't count the thing in Toco with his cousin) and never since, that Saturday evening when, bored or listless or drunk or fed up or stressed, they played All Fours late into the night and drank too much and he let Aloes convince him to stay the night and they collapsed onto his bed with its thin, cool mattress and soon, somehow, they were jerking each other off and suddenly Aloes was cupping Felix's ass, pulling down his buddy's track pants to just below his butt cheeks, spitting on his fingers and using them to moisten Felix's hole, moaning as he put his hard wood inside Felix, who kept saying fuck, fuck, fuck as Aloes pumped him with dick until Felix, on all fours, came all over the faded bedspread. They had kept the rest of their clothes on for the whole thing, as though removing them fully would have meant revealing something, would have changed the nature of the exchange from a transaction of convenience to one of intimacy.

The next day, they said nothing about it.

Nor the day after that.

But Felix would sometimes wake from sleep with the sensation that he had dreamt something that was too exquisite, too pleasurable to be remembered. He would breathe heavily and Jasmine would comfort him as though he had a nightmare. But Felix would always know it had not been a nightmare, that it had been a version of something too real, something he could never let come to light.

After the quick burial (there was no headstone), Felix heard someone mention the fact that Aloes was a drunk. He'd not been to work for a few days before the accident. The day it happened, he was driving from a rum shop in Siparia along a bad road. He lost control of the vehicle, they said.

But what if Aloes' death was no accident?

Felix had a good idea where the locusts were coming from. Leviathan Corp was doing more seismic surveys. Explosives had been detonated in the soil just outside the forest reserve to take measurements. Felix knew the shock from the explosions would have a domino effect, would topple trees, would traumatise wildlife, would disturb soil networks, would disrupt the balance. He was incensed. He tried his best not to think about of it. He tried his best to move on. To do what he needed to do:

find a way to support Jasmine and Max. To find a way to get his
job back. To find a way to carry on without Aloes. He needed
to clear his head.

When the locusts settled, it was as though his mind had
settled too. He knew what he was going to do with his
morning. He was going to drive. He needed to plan. He'd told
Jasmine nothing about his meeting with Minister Lashley. He
didn't mention that he'd been fired. Telling her would somehow make everything more real. And besides, he was working
on it. He drove out the driveway, his truck crunching locusts.

10.

At Moruga Beach, Felix stared out to sea. Gulls lined the water
like ticks in a ledger. Walking in the soft, warm sand, he
thought of Jasmine and Max. He thought of Aloes. Everything
seemed unbearable. A gull cried.

He was looking at chip chips in the sand, cold seawater
spraying his feet, when the thought occurred to him. It bright-
ened like a firefly in the dark.

Could it work? Could this plan work?

11.

On the road back to Pleasantville, Felix parked to the side. He
took out his phone and pulled up the pictures he'd once
planned to send to the Environmental Management Authority. He'd also planned to send them to a friend he knew in the
newspapers. Now he knew better. He deleted them.

Then, he dialled the number for the office of Minister of the
Environment, Arthur Lashley. He asked to speak to the Min-

ister's private secretary, the lady with the red jacket who had been so nice to him.

I have a very important message for the minister, Felix said. I need to see him urgently. Tell him it concerns an oil find that can turn the economy around.

12.

When forest rangers select a tree to be destroyed, they mark it. Felix walked up to the giant kapok tree under which he'd sheltered so many times and sprayed a bright orange X on it.

13.

A new oilrig was being built. Several surveys had found a mammoth reservoir of crude oil beneath the surface in an area that Felix pinpointed to the Ministry. As the new Conservator of Forests, replacing Mr Orville, Felix felt it important to show his face to supervise the clearing of what was previously designated an environmentally-sensitive area. The Minister and the new Conservator had been instrumental in getting that formal classification waived so the drilling could begin.

When Felix went back to the newly refurbished office at Pleasantville, it was bustling. There was now a team of twelve forest rangers. There had been a direct intervention from Minister Lashley to ensure proper staffing and resources. Felix gathered everyone into the new conference room for the morning briefing. They met every day like this to plan their enforcement activities. Confidently, Felix began the meeting:

So, fellas, how we going to get these hunters to comply with the law?

PRELUDES

2002

When I landed in London, leaves had started to fall from the trees. Our BWIA plane parked at Heathrow. I looked out the window and everything was ordinary and rundown but the terminal was huge. There was a chill. A baby on board was crying. I buttoned my new jumper. We got off the plane, mother and I.

They took me to the J2 section where they screen students coming to study. The lady at the counter had a strong Cockney accent. She shouted something at me but it took me a while until I figured out she was telling me to go through.

We got our luggage, got the shuttle to Euston, and then got a black cab to take us to Great Dover Street. The taxi driver asked if this was our first time in the UK. Mother beamed about how I had won a scholarship, was here to study law. She was just here to get me settled and make sure I had everything I needed. The taxi gave us a mini tour of the city and my eyes were glued on all that was unfolding outside the window. In the distance, the London Eye was a giant lollipop.

We filled out paperwork, got keys and settled into the apartment. My room was at the end of the corridor. There were three other rooms, but everything was quiet. Everything looked new and untouched. I was the first and I felt alone. Mother held my hand and I was glad she was there.

We unpacked a few things. Mother took out the crockery
and cutlery and a jar of classic yellow mustard. She figured
mustard would be a good thing to have in case we needed to
make a macaroni pie. It was odd to see her in the empty, white
kitchen. But I knew she felt this was her job as a parent – to fill
the new space with the colour of familiar things. We did a bit
of shopping at the green grocer's. Macaroni pie – a Trini
essential that I would later learn some British people called a
"pasta bake" – would be on the menu that first day. Despite my
protests, she made enough to last a week.

That first night, Mother slept on my bed. I slept in a sleeping
bag on the floor. I dreamt of everything I'd seen in the taxi, all
the scenes that seemed like the set of a movie: the London Eye,
Big Ben, Trafalgar Square, Piccadilly Circus, Oxford Street,
Waterloo Bridge, the Southbank, the slow-moving Thames,
the people everywhere – different people: different faces,
different clothes, different ways of walking and smoking and
talking and laughing and holding briefcases and holding hands.

★

Classes were on the Strand. I attended some lectures in a
baroque chapel with red walls and a pipe organ. Seminars were
in a tiny, cramped, brickstone building next to Somerset
House. Between classes, students would hang at the library on
Chancery Lane. I'd walk past the Royal Courts of Justice to get
to the lane. After studying in the library, I'd walk back over
Waterloo Bridge to halls. The sky would be a brilliant French
blue and planes would leave contrails as though spelling out
secret messages. The sun would begin to set and the city would
become one with its ochre light.

Mother left. There was so much to discover I didn't know
where to begin. One night, I went to Heaven, the gay club near
the university, and found I was only the second black person in
the room, which made me nervous. I hit the bar, soon learned

the proper name for a screwdriver was a "vodka orange", lingered around people for a bit. The men saw through and around me. Maybe it was because I was too twinky. Maybe it was because I was mixed. Maybe it was because I was from the Caribbean and they couldn't figure out where I was from. Walking home that night, a car pulled up and a man shouted Paki and sped away.

One summer, I got on a scheme to shadow a judge at a low-level court. But as soon as he saw me, he said he was sorry this would not work out and told me to go do something else instead. I wondered if he meant a career in law would not work out or simply that my shadowing him for the day would not work out. I was a little miffed, but it didn't bother me too much. I decided to walk around the courts to see what I could learn. I found out how trials worked that day. I was fascinated by one case in which the main witness was allowed to testify hidden behind a cloth screen, as though justice itself were a delicate piece of white fabric.

One of my roommates was gay, which could have been convenient. But Kurtz told me he wasn't into "Asian guys" and it was clear that he was referring to me. He had blond hair and blue eyes and several piercings. He was really thin and fixated on his appearance. Whenever he dated someone he found he didn't like, he was sure to introduce them to me as though we might make a great couple. But no one stuck around. I was looking for a true companion, someone who would walk hand in hand with me in the streets, shelter me in the rain with his umbrella.

In Trinidad I was never out. Not even Mother knew. The only person who was willing to admit that I might be gay was Godmother, but she lived far away in Texas. Every time she came to visit, and every time she rang me, which she did with alarming regularity I thought, she'd always sign off by saying,

"Remember Jesus loves the sinner, but he hates that sin." In London though, I could go to dinner parties and be free and it was fine. Or at least that was what I had thought in my head. That was what I had been led to believe, or allowed myself to believe, or wanted to believe, looking in from the outside, from my island afar.

The things people said at dinner parties, though! One lady once asked me, "Are there roads in Trinidad?" I thought this was a joke but she was serious. I told her the asphalt road in front of Buckingham Palace was paved with pitch from Trinidad, so yes, we have roads too. (Though privately I grumbled to myself that many of Trinidad's roads needed resurfacing). At another dinner party, people introduced me to a guy from Wales, who had an accent like mine. He was cute. He looked like the fella who played Frodo in *The Lord of the Rings*. I imagined us frolicking together in the shires, drinking ale and having picnics on sleepy hillsides. But he was really quiet and we didn't hit it off.

Two guys from separate seminars started flirting with me but for some reason I froze whenever they did. One guy was French and showed me a photo of his cute dog. Another was from Canada and, like me, he liked books . When I told him I was from Trinidad, he said he'd read Earl Lovelace's *The Schoolmaster* and I was impressed. But I didn't quite know what to do with all of this attention. I was always either oblivious or awkward. In some ways I was still a newcomer to myself, a tourist. I was present in this new world, but not all of me was prepared for it.

When I finally decided I was ready, I started chatting with Robert, a British guy from my criminal law seminar who looked like Hugh Grant. We went to the theatre to see Glenn Close in *A Streetcar Named Desire* and Brian Dennehy in *Death of a Salesman*. We went to the Tate Modern and stared into the painting by Dorothea Tanning of the girl being raped by a flower. We attended a screening of Pedro Almodóvar's *Bad Education* with Gael García Bernal. We saw Nicolas Roeg's *Don't Look Now* at a special screening and I held onto Robert's arm when the scary lady with the red coat appeared. One night, at a party at Robert's house, he got drunk and knelt before me and held my hand and kissed it and then got up and walked off to make out with this guy called Seamus.

I found out later they were boyfriends. They had been boyfriends all along. Seamus was also at King's but was studying English Literature which made me jealous of them both. I decided that was that and pulled out.

Soon after, one guy from my contract law seminar started walking with me to the library on Chancery Lane. He was sexy like George Michael in the 80s. He wore tight, distressed jeans. Had a cross earring. We'd chat among the law bookshops, window shop in front the luxury shirt stores, go for coffees at the tiny Starbucks that once operated on Chancery Lane. He was from Cyprus, and I think he felt kinship with me because of the island thing. After seminars one day I decided to ask him to go for a drink. We sat in a musky, wooden cubicle in The Cheshire Cat. He was telling me about how excited he was that Cyprus was going to join the EU when I put my hand on his hand and he recoiled. He looked at me with shock and disgust. He spat out that he wasn't gay. Then he got up and left. I headed to Heaven and got wasted.

The next morning, I had my first hangover on British soil. It was worse than any hangovers I'd had in Trinidad. At least in Trinidad it was always warm. Here the sky was a grey vault and I was sinking like an anchor into the cold waters of an icy river. This was the day, of all days, that I had to go to Forest Hill.

I was looking to bolster my CV so had volunteered to be a mentor in a school along with several students. According to the university, the programme involved reaching out to "inner city" kids, encouraging them to feel that it was possible to pursue a career in law. I didn't even know if I really wanted to be a lawyer or whether I'd come to London because I was gay and felt this was my chance to seek refuge from Trinidad.

The school at Forest Hill was warm and inviting. To me, the students all seemed so polite, the teachers so friendly. In the classrooms there were posters on all sorts of different things. One teacher was teaching the class about all of the religions of the world, with posters about the Bhagavad Gita, the Quran, and the Bible side by side. Suddenly I felt at ease; I felt this could be a classroom anywhere in Trinidad. I enjoyed my chat with Peter, my mentee, who was way too tall for his age. He had a huge head of curly hair and said he wanted to be a novelist or a filmmaker when he grew up. I smiled. I think I finally saw myself.

Walking out the school, someone called out my name.

Finn!

A car drove up beside me. It was Robert. I'd forgotten he would be here. He offered a lift. I hesitated. We hadn't spoken since the night of his party. But I was tired. A lift wouldn't hurt.

The awkward silence was painful. Before, we used to have such an easy way of talking with one another. Now that comforting camaraderie was gone. I began to regret accepting his lift.

Then, Robert said, Did you know Raymond Chandler lived here in Forest Hill? And I grinned because he remembered Chandler was one of my favourite writers. Suddenly it felt good to be in a car driving along unfamiliar roads with a friend. It was early evening, chilly but not too much, and we saw trees that had turned red, orange and gold. We saw blackbirds on fences, and pigeons on old buildings. There were houses and gardens and libraries and museums.

And by the time we got back to the centre of the city I felt better once more, hopeful once more. I could hear my heart beating. I could hear Robert's breathing. I could hear the whole city's noise as we sat there in the dark of the car on the street waiting for me to say goodnight and go inside.

1989

Everything was wrong. I woke that morning with a sense of dread. The sun rose and it was my own fear rising. I knew something bad was about to happen.

Father was moody once more. He ate breakfast at the table silently. The night before there had been a quarrel about the bank again. Mother said something, then Father said something, then the silence said something, a silence that fell on the house like a blanket of vexness. It covered everything, was louder than them both and extended its tendrils deep into the night as we all exhaled, my sisters and I, on our cool beds.

I went outside. I cleaned the kennels and walked up the back steps. Longdenville sprawled before me, a collage of rusty roofs and asphalt roads, mottled with green treetops. From these steps, on good days, I felt the world was in front of me. Everything was ahead and all of this Trinidadian landscape was part of some runway leading to another future. Today, though, the sun climbed high in the sky like a curse.

Mom made tea and I packed my sandwich for school then went to have a shower. The bathroom tiles felt cold, the water was colder. When I finished, I walked past my father in the corridor. He looked at me as though looking at a stranger walking through his house. I shut my bedroom door. Then it happened.

What struck me most about the way Father called me into

the living room was how ordinary his voice was. There were no hysterics. No cursing. No smashing of plates against the wall. No threats or recriminations. He just came out and said it:

Why do you wear your towel on your chest like a woman?

Don't you ever do that again, Finn.

Bring me the wooden spoon.

I wondered what he wanted to do with a wooden spoon, since I'd never seen Father cook. And I wondered what all the fuss was about with the towel. I wore my towel the way my older sisters did. It was too long to drape around my waist, wouldn't it drag against the floor?

When he hit me with the wooden spoon I thought of Shirley, our dog, in the kennel outside. I thought of the way she had licked me earlier that day, as though licking some wound that was to come.

2006

I came straight from the airport. When we turned off the road, the taxi drove through a thicket of almond trees. It was night time and the taxi's lights cast shadows that made the trees multiply. Soon, I could see the house at the edge of the cliff. And already, what had been a memory came roaring back at me. The sea: booming, murmuring, overwhelming. Fresh sea breeze blew into the car.

I had come back to live on the island. My family was expecting me at Longdenville (this was before I moved to Woodbrook), but first I would stay here for a few days. A welcome home gift to myself.

Trevor, for that was the name on the card he gave me, parked the taxi at the front of the beach house. I asked him to wait while I opened up. I had keys. We had picked them up from the housekeeper along the way. I had stayed at this house before. I had told the housekeeper there was no need for him to come with me at this hour of the night. He said the house was aired and there were a few basics in the fridge. I noticed the outside light, which worked with a timer, was not on. As I fumbled in the carport for the switch, I noticed the foul stench. I flipped the switch but the bulb did not light. I stumbled over something heavy. I ran back into the open yard where there was moonlight.

Trevor brought a torch. I suddenly saw how attractive he was.

We followed the beam of light back into the carport. The dead dog revealed itself. Its throat was slit. Blood had caked into molasses and oozed out of the wound. Little rice grains, maggots, crawled from its mouth. Its blood dyed a burlap bag revealing its tightly woven threads. There was a trail of blood. Someone had dragged the dead dog here from the front yard over the pale gravel. I followed this trail, but it vanished in the direction of the neighbour's house where I knew a few kids lived.

Trevor started the car and I thought he was leaving but he was really turning the car around to direct its beams onto the garage.

It seemed like an ominous sign. It didn't match with anything I was feeling inside. I had been longing to return for so long. On mornings in London, I would wake up in my dreary, cramped lodging at Crouch End, and imagine the sweet aroma of a tropical sun-ripened mango. Not the garbage they had in Sainsbury's. I would hear the wind rustling through the trees in our yard in Longdenville. I missed our mango tree, our coconut tree, our sour cherry tree, the pommecythere, the neighbour's cashew tree, the ten-pound zabocas that would hang and sway like mute, green church bells. For many months,

I would ring Enrico – who would always pick up the phone during his shifts at Wendy's – and cry into the receiver. It didn't help that things hadn't worked out with Robert. Nor did they work out with Roger. Nor Hanson. Nor Charlie. Even online hookups were tough, a sea of rejection: No Asians, No Blacks, No Femmes, No Fats, No offence but not into Arabs (?). At bars I was chronically shy and people would ignore me when I mustered the courage to make conversation. Those people I did manage to bed consumed me only because they felt I was rare and exotic in some way. They could see no further than that. I had believed that leaving Trinidad would set me free. Instead, I became invisible. When Enrico sent the job vacancy he saw for a firm near him in Woodbrook, it was a simple decision. I wanted Trinidad. I had to come back.

But now, looking at this dead dog, I wondered.

I wanted Trinidad but did Trinidad want me? I suddenly felt incredibly tired and jet lagged.

Trevor said he'd come with me inside the house with the torchlight. There was no power. If someone had been here recently, I could not tell. Nothing was disturbed. No air had entered for months. There was a musty, dank smell. There were thick chunky candles and matches in a kitchen drawer that I lit, revealing dust and cobwebs and I wondered if Miss Havisham lived here. A pile of old magazines was strewn on the coffee table. Twigs and clove-like droppings indicated bats. I opened a window. I opened the doors to the veranda overlooking the cliff. Sea breeze rushed in, beastly and magnificent. Trevor stood next to me looking out at the vastness. The full moon lit a white, sparkling path leading to some place beyond the night.

I'll help you, he said.

We each took a corner of the bag and dragged it. The dog felt unyielding, as though a powerful magnet was pulling it deep into the earth. Had it been someone's pet? It looked like one of those feral country dogs that roamed the streets. We took it far away to a part of the cliff where the soil was soft, but not too soft, under some coconut trees. The breeze here was powerful, but the stench remained. We had a fork and spade from the garage and took turns digging. We turned to the sea now and then and took in big gulps of air. In the moonlight, Trevor took off his shirt and suddenly, through this close proximity, the shock of our shared labour, I got a real sense of him: how he moved, how tall he was, how broad his shoulders were, the shapeliness of his limbs. We put the dog in the pit and started to cover it with soil. I took my shirt off too. Our bodies glistened with sweat. I could hear the engine of the surf hissing as though it was powered by hot steam. Eventually, the task was done. Strangely, in burying something, I felt something else had been unearthed.

I have rum in my carry-on, I said.

Good, I need a drink real bad, he said.

I remembered there was an outdoor shower at the back of the house. I found some blue soap. I let him go first. In the murk, I could see him take off all of his clothes as though he had done so in front of me several times before. The pipe sputtered then exploded when he turned on the tap. As the water hit him, he moaned. Then he beckoned me to come.

The pressure real good, he said.

The water was cool, cold almost, and the pressure of the jet from the nozzle was sharp and bruising, firing thousands of hard pearls at my flesh. I gasped. He laughed. And then he soaped me, casually, easily, as though we had done this some time before and were used to it. His casualness emboldened me. I held him. He kissed me. And it was as though I was swallowing the night sky with its diamond stars, the black ocean with its orange welts of oil rigs in the distance, the spidery coconut trees dancing their shadow ballet against the moon, the sea foam and the sea spray, the memory of the dead dog, of death, my desire to come home – it was as though it was all filling me. I drank in his salty taste. I held his dick in my hand, and felt I was holding some heavy fruit, some memory, some dream.

We never opened the rum.

★

The housekeeper knocked on the door. I jumped up in bed, startled. I was alone in the small bedroom. I was naked among a creased sea of crumpled sheets. I found my trousers and, inspecting myself in the mottled mirror, tried to look unsexed.

Sorry about the power, the housekeeper said when I got outside. I fixed the problem.

I saw Trevor' taxi was not in the yard. A wave of sadness crashed on the rocks inside me. I dug into my trouser pockets. I found the card he had given me. With my hand still in my pocket, I held onto the card as though holding a memory. I continued the conversation with the housekeeper, telling him about the dog.

It was that miserable child next door, he said without hesitation. He's been killing things all week. I'll speak with the mother again. Kids these days, yes, they watching all that Harry Potter sorcery stupidness.

★

When the housekeeper left, when I was finally alone, the world around me settled into something unreal. Memories of the night before came back: how we had kissed; how I had trailed my tongue from his lips to his ears to his neck and then down to his left nipple, down along his chest; how I had knelt before him and swallowed the entirety of his wet cock; how we had somehow made it to the bedroom, dusting off the bed; how I lay on my back as he parted my legs then lifted them up towards my head; how I could hear waves crashing as he pounded me until I came; how we lay arm in arm before falling asleep. For a moment, these memories mixed with my elation at being home. But then disappointment overcame me because what had happened, the whole ordeal with the dog, the way the entire encounter had seemingly brought us together, had ended so easily with the sunrise. Trevor had told me he lived in Carenage with his sister and his mom. Would I ever see him again? There was a number on the card. I told myself I would ring him later (my phone had died in the night).

The house appeared oddly clean, cleaner than it had been last night, as though someone had removed a heavy filter from an image and allowed us to see what was there all along. The place was organ-warm, pulsing. Pure sunlight, sunlight as clear as white wine, burst through the windows, through the veranda doors, through the little holes left for wind to enter. A breeze was blowing. Birds sang. I had no idea what time it was. I went into the yard.

I saw it.

The taxi hadn't gone as I had thought. He'd gotten up early, parked it discretely at the side of the house.

I walked down the worn, rocky steps, pieces of which had been interchanged over the years like some kind of Frankenstein construction. They led to the small bay beneath the house. All in front of me, the aquamarine waves beckoned, their alternating allegro and adagio speaking of some happiness to come.

And there he was, on the sand, walking towards me.

MS.

1.

The Petit Valley Writing Club had, for the moment, three members. But what it lacked in size, it made up for in enthusiasm. Meetings were held, religiously, on the first and third Saturday of every month, and there were "Extraordinary Meetings" on public holidays. Sometimes, emergency writing sessions would be convened if one member of the group was having a bad week. On these occasions, Iris, Amber and Esmeralda would meet and write together for hours, often late into the night. Writing was a way to escape the stress and chaos of the world. They clung to the fact that they shared the same passion for words and stories, a passion that they thought was somewhat unusual for people of their youth. This was not a group of friends who celebrated milestones or achievements by throwing wild pool parties or going to fetes. Their idea of a good lime was sitting down around a table in front of their laptops and responding to ingenious writing prompts – often devised by Iris, the club's founder – while sipping from hot, sugary cups of coffee and eating cupcakes.

Iris' house on Orchid Drive was normally the scene of these sessions, but occasionally, just to change things up, the group liked to go to the café on Morne Coco Road (with the chocolate zuccini muffins that Amber so relished). Or they might chose a spot somewhere in nearby Woodbrook or Maraval or the ice-cream place around the Savannah. Once, at Esmeralda's suggestion, they even went to the National Library in downtown Port of Spain, but the WiFi was so bad and the parking so atrocious they resolved never to meet there again.

They felt more excited than usual about their next session; they were meeting at their favourite Rituals in Maraval and a new member was joining the club: a friend of Iris' younger brother Ben. He had been their fourth member, but had taken a job teaching English in Japan. Before he left, he recommended his buddy, a guy named Finn, as a possible replacement.

Do you know what Susie told me last week? Amber said as they waited for the new guy. That bitch claimed no man would ever want to be with a writer like me because, and I quote, *Having a writer as a partner is the worst thing imaginable.*

I mean, I can kinda see her point, Esmeralda said.

What? No, how can you say that? Iris said.

Think about it, Esmeralda said. Nothing sucks more than having a writer as a friend. One: everything, *everything* you tell us ends up in a story. Two: we are forever asking people to read our latest piece, be it a short story or, worse, book-length manuscript. Three: Iris and Amber you are both so generous and supportive of me and I love your feedback, but, let's be honest, there are writers out there who cannot take an ounce of criticism. So imagine having to live with that. I tell Roshan absolutely nothing about my writing, *nothing*.

I guess you have some valid points there, Iris said.

Amber continued to fume: Susie said she heard stories of published authors getting vex if you didn't buy their latest book. Can you imagine? Is that true? Are there really writers out there like that?

Listen, that's why I'm glad I'm friends with you guys, Iris said, we're just way more chill than these serious literary types, aren't we?

Amber and Esmeralda nodded assent but privately remembered the group's fight, a few days prior, over V.S. Naipaul. Iris had been passionately in favour of the comedy and heart of Naipaul's early books like *Miguel Street* and *A House for Mr Biswas,* and Amber and Esmeralda had been up in arms against his depiction of women and gays in later books like *Guerillas* and *In a Free State.* Iris had argued that they should, after Roland Barthes, separate the work from the writer. Amber and Esmeralda insisted such a separation was an artificial construct designed to placate and nullify legitimate calls for accountability. So heated had the discussion become that, when the waiter came up to take their orders in the little café on Tragarete Road, they forgot to place their customary requests for coffee and assorted cakes.

Finn, a short man wearing a white shirt with rolled-up sleeves and brown corduroy trousers, approached their table. He carried a grey man-bag within which he had his laptop and a few notepads. The group exchanged introductions, with Iris saying how pleased she was that he could join them and mentioning how much she had heard about him from her brother, who spoke so highly of him. Finn, who seemed a little sweaty, replied that he had heard so much about them too and was really looking forward to getting to share his work with them. He was working on a manuscript of short stories and would be so grateful for any feedback. He had been so busy at work and had not been able to write as much as he wanted, but that had changed and he was now between jobs and spending more time at home in Woodbrook. Sensing Finn might be nervous at meeting new people, Iris quickly devised an "icebreaker" for the group that would also double as the creative writing exercise for today's meeting. The exercise was simple.

Write a story in ten minutes, she said. Any setting. Any theme. Anything at all. Just do it in ten minutes. Sometimes, all you need to write, especially if you've not been writing for a while, is just for someone to say *Write!*

Ten minutes later, they shared each other's pieces.

Iris wrote a poetic passage describing a drive to the beach, with vivid descriptions of poui trees in the distance. Amber wrote a short story set in the 1930s on a cocoa estate in which a woman was having a passionate affair. Esmeralda presented what she described as "fragments": one in which she was feeding her dog, another a dream about snakes, and a third about tending to her garden. When it was Finn's turn to present, he read this story:

Closing Time

Fifteen minutes after he took their orders the waiter came back.

Sorry, are you guys writers?

The two people looked up from their laptops to check where the voice came from. His hair was untidy. His nametag crooked. Instead of Roger, which had been scratched out, Finnegan was pencilled in.

The coffee shop was about to close. There were only a few customers. A Nina Simone CD was playing on loop.

Yes, I'm a writer, said Diana. And so is my friend.

Cool. I write too. Have you written books?

We've written a few.

Oh really? Which ones?

I've written a historical novel about the Amerindians, Diana said. Do you write?

I'm writing a novel. Nothing special. Just personal things. About boys mostly. Maybe I could show you guys? I'm working on a new chapter and it would be great to get feedback.

Sure.

Finnegan disappeared into the kitchen.

Diana sipped the last of her coffee. It was good. She looked out the window. It was getting dark. The bank across the street was closed. The street vendors were gone. Streetlights began to come on. People were driving in and out of the KFC and the gym.

We can't back out now, Nick said.

Diana heard him speak but did not respond. She stared at his eyebrows. Thick, dark. He should get them plucked; they stick out too much, draw too much attention.

We have to change the plan, she said. She counted how many people were still inside. Just two. And one of them looked like he was about to leave. She reached for her gun in her handbag.

When Finnegan returned they were gone.

★

I absolutely love that story! Iris said. You had me hooked from the very first sentence –

And that gun! Amber said.

Oh my god that gun, Esmeralda echoed. She adjusted her large handbag self-consciously.

It's really amazing how you took our real life café setting and turned it into such a compelling story, Iris said. Down to the Nina Simone music! That detail about the guy's eyebrows was so funny too.

You definitely need to continue this, Amber said.

Yes, you have to continue this, Esmeralda repeated.

Finn expressed gratitude for the positive feedback and suggested he might think about adding the piece to his manuscript.

2.

For the next meeting, members were asked to share something new they had been working on. Iris shared a story about
a picnic in the Savannah, with vivid descriptions of flamboy-
ant trees in the distance. Amber shared an extract from a
lengthy work-in-progress, a historical novel about a leper
colony down the islands for which she had done far too much
research. Esmeralda apologised; she'd been so busy at the
bank and it had been hard to prepare anything for the meeting. Finn shared a story about a security guard at a school who
discovers a student has been squatting in the compound. It
began:

Night Class

The May Fair was over, the lights turned off, the bran
tub emptied, the decorations taken down and locked in
cupboards safely. The bouncy castle stood still, await-
ing the workmen who would remove it tomorrow. The
gates to the schoolyard were shut and the sentry assumed duty.

No one saw the boy in black. He hid inside a cabinet
in the horror house until the last of the crowds had
gone. When it was completely dark, he slipped out of
the school and into the yard. From a distance, he looked
at the guard booth. He got closer, peeping through the
iron louvres of the small concrete shed. A bright lamp
glowed, but the sentry was asleep again. He reclined in
his comfortable chair; a portable radio was on and
dreamy voices from another country drifted into the
night...

★

I loved the part when the guard sees the child and thinks it's a douen, Iris said.

And that ending! Amber said. Your endings are amazing. The tension builds up so strongly in this one. And then it releases when we realise nothing bad is going to happen.

It was so cool of the guard to not report the boy, Esmeralda said. And that detail about how the boy reminded the guard about his son living in Germany said so much about our world today!

Finn said the story was from his MS., which he was now calling *Surfacing and Other Stories*, and that the story was inspired by something that happened in real life to his father, who was once a security guard.

That's incredible! Iris enthused.

3.

The next meeting was supposed to be dedicated entirely to improvised writing exercises (Iris had formulated one prompt based on the colour pink). However, Finn said he had a new story that he was eager to get off his chest and share. It began:

Valentine's Day

That night, all I could see in my mind was the razor. Glimmering, pristine, its sharp edge as thin as a blade of grass. I got up and walked to the bathroom. I looked in the mirror and came to terms with the fact that I was alone. On Valentine's Day. Again. I took off my shirt.

In the mirror, my scars were now so thick, so encrusted, that my forearms appeared slathered in a thick caramel, by now so scarred with constant slicing that the flesh no longer seemed like flesh but rather some kind of inhuman substance.

I found the satchel in which I kept my blade and opened it. There it was, like a puppy sleeping in its bed. I took it out.

Then, I put the blade to my arm and felt the relief coursing out of me. My arms tingled with need, their circuitry fizzing and blipping with electricity. I felt the creature inside me sit up, aware of danger but unable to escape it. For so long I had wanted this creature inside me to tuck itself into a sleep from which it would never awake. For so long I'd failed and the creature had always come back. I looked at the man in the mirror. I again drew the razor across my arm...

★

The rest of the story consisted entirely of increasingly vivid and alarming descriptions of self-harm. Finn smiled when he came to the story's end.

Those descriptions of cutting are so good! Amber said. It's almost as though we are right there in the room with – but then she suddenly realised the implication: the possibility that Finn had written this story based on, yet again, something personal.

Iris thought to ask, as diplomatically as possible, whether the story was based on a real-life experience, but then ruled the question out. If it was autobiographical, and Finn *was* harming himself, it would be insensitive to ask him so bluntly. She decided to focus on something else.

Is this going to be in *Surfacing and Other Stories* too?

Finn said the story would definitely be a part of the collection and that his manuscript was advancing well, especially since he remained at home most days (he was still between jobs) and had nothing to do but write. He was working on even more stories like this, he added.

Esmeralda said nothing, but she carefully scanned Finn's arms for any signs of a scar or any clue that he might be cutting himself. He was in a white shirt again today. But she noticed his sleeves were not rolled up as usual.

4.

Everyone was worried when Finn emailed his next story the day before that week's meeting.

Did you read Finn's story? Amber asked Iris over the phone.

Amber, I can't talk right now, Iris said. I'm at work. Can we chat about this later?

READ FINN'S STORY, Amber said and hung up.

During her lunch break Iris pulled up the group email with the story attached. It began:

The Worker

These nights, the streets of Woodbrook are quiet. I do my best to keep my head down. You never know when the police are going to come. You have to blend in. You have to disappear. Which is fitting because, in a way, I've already disappeared.

You can tell when a trick's looking. There's this way they slow down and creep alongside you. Sometimes a car might drive right past, at normal speed, and there's no sign that they want you. But then later, maybe minutes, maybe hours, after they've worked up the courage, they come back.

Sometimes, I can tell just by looking at a guy's face

whether he's going to be one of the shy guys or one of the wicked ones. But sometimes, I'm off. Once, a nice guy drove me to Carenage, parked on the beach, played with my totee and asked me to suck him off. But then, after he came in my mouth, he zipped his fly back up and told me to get out of the car. No money. No drop back to Woodbrook. When I confronted him, he banged my head against the car window. Then, he pushed me out of the car and drove off, leaving me bleeding on the rocky shoreline. My body was shaking. I felt liquid oozing all over my face. I remembered the pain of my head hitting the glass. The beach smelt of sour milk and dead animals. I don't remember how I got home. But sometimes, in my dreams, I think of men like that guy. I think of all the tricks who've mistreated me. I imagine finding out where they live. Who their wives are. What they do for work. I don't imagine confronting them. No. I imagine taking a bull pistle whip and beating them. I imagine their screams of agony. I imagine their desperate pleas for mercy as I kick and stamp and spit on them. I imagine their bodies black and bruised. I imagine them dead...

★

Iris closed the story and immediately started a new text chain with everyone in the club except Finn.

IRIS: U guys really think just cause he's written a story about a prostitute that he's a prostitute now and wants to kill people???

AMBER: I'm saying we all know he's been having a hard time. I'm telling you this story feels completely biographical. We need to do something. He's crying out for our help!

IRIS: But what if he just likes to write dark stories? They

don't have to be real. I mean didn't he say the other day that he was reading lots and lots of books these days? What was the book he mentioned? *A Little Life*? *The End of Eddy*? Maybe it's what he's reading that's influencing him?

ESMERALDA: Yes but WHY would he be reading books like that?

AMBER: Come on Iris, ALL of his stories so far have been veiled disguises of real life. Remember the one where he simply changed his name from Finn to Finnegan?

ESMERALDA: That story was creepy!

IRIS: Yes, but we can't know for sure…

AMBER: Why don't you ask Ben what he knows about this guy?

IRIS: Okay, I'll ask him. But because of the time difference to Japan it might take me a few days to get a reply. See you all tmrw.

Iris understood where the group was coming from. She'd had thoughts like theirs before about Finn's work. But at the same time, she was a strong believer in the ideas of Barthes, whom she had read on her literature course away at King's College London, and believed speculation about an author's life should not get in the way of appreciating his work (she frequently quoted from 'Death of the Author' at club meetings). Not only might such speculation be wrong, it was irrelevant to the separate living thing represented by the text. She thought, too, of Oscar Wilde, another of her favourite writers. All art is at once surface and symbol, he said. It is the spectator, and not life, that art really mirrors. Was the group really seeing Finn, or were they seeing something else?

But that night, Iris woke from her sleep because in her dreams she remembered yet another quote from another of her favourite writers. Naipaul himself had said: An autobiography can distort; facts can be realigned. But fiction never lies. It reveals the writer totally.

5.

The next day, Finn arrived completely oblivious to the crisis he had provoked. He wore his usual white shirt, which was crisp and clean and neatly tucked into his trousers. Iris and Amber watched him munch a slice of coconut sweetbread as he discussed his writing process with geeky glee (Esmeralda had excused herself from the meeting saying she was busy that day). His voice was gentle, his manner so meek. Iris thought the gap between the person before them and the narrator of the story was so large that it was a clear sign that the men in the stories were not him. At the same time, maybe the difference showed what an expert he was at hiding his true self. Still, she couldn't picture Finn on the streets at night picking up tricks and then turning into a vengeful murderer.

It's not real, she whispered to Amber when Finn went to the bathroom.

But when Finn came back from the bathroom, he was all bright-eyed and excited. He said he had just got a brilliant idea. He would rename his manuscript *My Life: An Autobiography in Stories*. That way, it would feel like a more personal project. All the stories would have a clear connection or link. He tentatively suggested he might finally send them the entire manuscript soon.

Iris and Amber looked at each other with alarm, but mumbled something about the title being a great idea and yes they would love to read his short story collection.

6.

It turned out Iris's brother Ben couldn't shed much light on the situation. In a long email to Iris the week after, Ben explained how Finn was a friend of an old schoolmate; how Ben was really friends with that schoolmate, not Finn *per se*; how, as a result, Ben wasn't sure whether Finn would be likely to open up to him if he was going through some kind of distress or financial difficulty; how their mutual schoolmate had averred that he had known Finn as a child at secondary school but, in the years since, had not kept in touch and that he and Finn were only recently reacquainted and therefore not close.

Iris was disappointed but also relieved. Lack of information meant lack of confirmation of Amber and Esmeralda's outlandish theory. Just because nobody really knew Finn didn't mean he was doing all the things his characters were doing in his writing. She felt justified in maintaining course and keeping things as they were, though she began to make a special effort to be friendly with Finn in order to understand his life situation and to glean whether there was any secret torment going on in his heart.

7.

Fifteen years later, there was a huge crowd gathered at the Old Fire Station in downtown Port of Spain for the Bocas Lit Fest, the country's annual literary festival.

The Old Fire Station was stone-built, with well-articulated cornerstones, a tower that gave nice a view of the city, and huge windows whose ledges had piped edges that looked like pink frosting. The building was now used almost exclusively for literary events. Tonight, the crowd was present to see one person: Finn Singh, the renowned Trinidadian author, whose fourth novel, *Living Proof*, had just been published to local and international acclaim.

What an absolutely delightful reading Mr Singh, the moderator, the journalist Marina Selvon, said. Thank you so much for sharing that wonderfully hilarious passage from your book. I think everyone will agree with me that you have such a gift for injecting joy and humour into your writing, even when you touch serious topics. Since we have a few more minutes to spare, I'd just like to ask one final question: Where does your inspiration come from?

Inspiration can come from many places, Finn said. It can come from a newspaper clipping. It can come from a book I've read. It can come from a story I've heard. I think to be a good writer you have to be a good observer of the world. So much so that when you set pen to paper, you have to be able to convince the reader that the story you are telling is, in fact, your story. Sometimes you do draw from your own life, but it gets messy because you might only take certain things, certain snippets, and put together this hodgepodge that somehow magically becomes its own thing. But it would be both right and wrong to feel you can assume everything a writer writes is taken from their personal experience. I can actually tell a funny story about this. When I was starting out as a writer, I was in this wonderful writing club where we'd meet up and share each other's stories and give feedback to one another. I remember in those days I was so moody and depressed as a human being. This was years ago. I was a single, under-sexed, unemployed gay man living in Woodbrook. I used to write these whack, violent stories – I remember I once wrote one about a drug addict castrating himself, can you imagine? – and apparently people in the club actually began to think that everything I was writing was real, that I had, for instance, become hooked on opium and was prostituting myself at nights. I wish! That would have been more fun. Years later, one of the writers in the group (we are all still in touch) told me they had been so worried they were about to stage some kind of dramatic intervention over tea. Then, when I met my boyfriend, who is here tonight – stand up Salvador for them to see you! – suddenly my stories became much lighter; suddenly I was writing about boring people like poets and mathematicians and chess players and what have you and everything had pretty sunsets and flowers blossoming and hummingbirds drinking nectar. And basically, it was all because I was finally getting laid!

The room filled with laughter.

Umm, what a wonderful note to end on! the moderator said. Ladies and gentlemen, let's show our appreciation one more time for Mr Finn Singh, author of *Living Proof*, which, by the way, you may purchase at the desk in the back. There was a hearty round of applause. Then everyone rose and began to make their way to the next event.

NOT LOOKING

1.

The day I finally gave up on my novel, I slept with Dorian.
There was no connection between the two things. That's just
how it happened.

When I let him in the front door, Buster barked as though
a bandit had broken in. It was strange. Dorian had been over
many times before and Buster had always been indifferent.
He'd been unimpressed by Dorian's attempts to charm him.
He'd sniff him a little with a bored look, then slink back to his
nook under my writing desk. I put him in the linen closet at the
end of the hall, and guided Dorian to my bedroom.

The Dorian thing was complicated. Some weeks before, he
had started visiting me just to chat. We knew each other yet
didn't know each other. We had mutual friends, but not
enough to matter. When he was single, I was in a relationship.
When I was single, he was taken. I always thought he liked me,
though I was confused as to why. He was a good-looking guy.
He was from Diego Martin. He worked as a social media
manager for a local Carnival band. He dressed like the other
white boys you see in North West Trinidad – perpetually in
flip-flops and board shorts. He had this poetic Kurt Cobain
vibe and a surfer-dude body that made me think he'd walked
straight out of *Point Break*.

We first met at an ice-cream parlour in Maraval. He was

ahead of me in the line and couldn't decide between the Funfetti Vanilla Sundae or the Nutella Chocolate Cone. I told him to get what I always got: the Peanut Butter and Jelly Orgasm. Then I felt embarrassed because I hadn't intended to come over as flirtatious. He didn't seem to make anything of it. We spent that afternoon chatting. In those days, Dorian was looking to make new friends. Before going our separate ways, we decided to keep in touch. I thought it was a nice afternoon and that was that.

But Dorian was serious about staying in touch. At his suggestion, we ended up going to a few overpriced, artsy events. That was the kind of thing people in his circle did in those days, go to "art things" where they would circulate and sip wine and eat cheese and gossip voraciously about their fellow artists. It wasn't my scene.

Nothing else happened between us. And I wasn't entirely sure I wanted anything to happen. Whenever it looked as though we might move beyond the friend zone, whenever it seemed maybe the conversation was getting genuinely deep, we would stumble and never quite make it over the finish line. As the weeks went by, Dorian became increasingly unresponsive to my texts. Then, I became preoccupied with reorganising my life after quitting my job. I moved on. Sometimes he called but I would miss the call and genuinely forget to call back.

One day, during lockdown, Dorian messaged to say he needed my help. He had quit his job at the mas camp in order to go to university abroad, but then those plans got blitzed by the pandemic. So now he was just home all day and was applying for jobs. He needed references. That's where I came in. But he didn't want me as a referee. He wanted me to help draft glowing testimonials for people to sign. I told him sure, why not.

He came with a laptop but never opened it. He talked about his family. He talked about the generations and generations of dastardly betrayals that had lead up to this point: his life of unemployment and desperate penury – all of which he endured from the confines of his parent's townhouse. He talked about his wonderful female friends. He talked about all of the enemies he had made in the local arts community. He said he was no longer interested in being part of "the gay scene" because it bothered him that there was so much bacchanal. People were forever falling in love with him. Too much drama. He had stories to tell. Loads and loads of stories. People were disgusting. So now, all his friends were straight. And he was living a life of abstinence. He was happy being single. He was not looking, not looking at all. But as he spoke, I couldn't help but wonder if the opposite was true. I was riveted.

This was how our conversations started. Sometimes he'd come over and I'd order pizza and we'd chat for hours. Other times, we'd talk on the phone, and I'd lie flat on my back in bed and just talk because I couldn't focus on anything else whenever I spoke with him. He had a lot of issues. His conversations required your undivided attention. Or at least that's how they seemed to me.

We talked about politics (he said he was a feminist and had no interest in lobbying for gay rights), we talked about our favourite albums, we talked about our exes, we talked about sex. After he got a job working remotely for a telemarketing company, we started shopping together. He had specific things he needed to buy. Because I'd spend my days cooped up working on the novel, I jumped at the chance to leave the house. I didn't have a dime, but he had a cute blue jeep. One day, he turned up at my door and took me for a drive just because he wanted to talk. We drove to Fort George and watched the sun set, came back to my place and talked some more. Then he hugged me and left.

I told my flatmate Granderson about all of this. Granderson wasn't the most talkative of people but he made a whole speech about how life is short and Dorian was obviously into me and if he was spending so much time with me maybe I should give it a try.

No way, I said, he's way too young and confused and besides he's not looking. I'm not looking.

Yeah, but that's how it happens. He's only four years younger than you. What do you have to lose?

You know what he told me the other day? He said he never makes the first move because then if anything happens it's not his fault. How stupid is that?

He's just afraid to make the first move, so what? Help him out. Do something to take things up a notch.

It happened easily enough. The first step of my seduction was to grow a beard. Dorian had a weakness for older men. Which meant he was into daddies. My new beard gave me an Ernest Hemingway vibe, if we picture Ernest Hemingway as a nerdy dougla from Woodbrook who was struggling to complete his first novel after unceremoniously leaving his job as a paralegal. I toned my body. I did kickboxing as much as I could, thinking all the while of my old boss who'd pushed me out because she didn't like my "lifestyle".

Next, I stopped calling him. Men prefer it if someone gives them space. That space is a form of control for them: it allows them to feel like they are setting the pace. It never occurs to them that someone who is submissive could be in charge.

The day I decided to abandon my long-suffering novel, he messaged to say he was having a rough day. His boss at the telemarketing company was a jerk.

Why don't you come over? I said. I'll cook something bland and tasteless.

You're such a racist, he said. Okay, I'll be there in an hour.

I closed the word processor file. Clicked the icon and dragged it to the little trash can. Then I selected "Empty Trash". My laptop made a loud sound, and Buster looked up as if asking me if I was sure. And something lifted in me, as though I had freed myself from a trap I'd been trying to escape for many years.

Later that evening, when I guided him to my bedroom, Dorian marvelled at all the fairy lights I'd strung up. It was a cool and rainy night. I told him he could sit on my bed. He could lay down. We could just relax and not talk. He didn't flinch as I lay down beside him. I rolled to my side, held him.

What is happening? he said, but he made room for me, made room for my arms.

Shut up, I said. We cuddled each other.

When I got hard, I made sure to press my body into him so he could feel it. We stayed like that for a while. Then he started stroking my arm, which felt like the closest thing to a signal he would ever give me. I kissed him and as my tongue pushed into the softness of his mouth I felt a new space opening between us, a cavern that was dark but gleaming, studded with spectacular crystals, like the inside of the brilliant cave I had dreamt about as a boy the day my father died.

2.

I got stuck writing my novel because of what was happening in the news.

My writing was all light and sunshine, all about happiness and positivity. My characters were gay. I wanted to give them happy lives and happy endings. They had happy families, happy relationships. They didn't die of AIDS. They didn't get bashed to death by homophobic thugs while walking the streets. They weren't molested by priests. I wanted to write something different for them. I wanted something more.

But the news just wouldn't let me.

First, came the murder of a prominent businessman, whom the papers said "had never married" but who was well known in the LGBTQ community. He was found stabbed to death in his elegant townhouse in Maraval.

Then came the actor, famous for his hilarious comedies, who was found dead in his living room in what police described as an "apparent robbery attempt". The headline in one paper the next day was "NO ONE'S LAUGHING NOW".

Then my drag queen friend Asha was beaten outside the Port of Spain General Hospital by some asshole. She posted pictures of her bruises on Facebook and I couldn't even message her.

There were other reports. There were rumours. In recent years there had been a string of unsolved stabbings, each involving men who were understood to be gay or on the down low. The chef stabbed in Woodbrook, the florist stabbed in San Fernando, the jogger found dead in the Savannah with stab wounds, the hotel manager thrown, bound and gagged, off Lady Young Road, his body badly punctured. People began to wonder if these incidents were linked. The whispers in the community were to the effect that there was someone targeting gay men, that there might even be a serial killer.

I escaped to my novel. I gave my characters great jobs. They didn't have bosses or co-workers who didn't like the fact that they were queer. No one fired them under false pretences. There were no lawyers who pressured their clerks to quit by overloading them with work. No one denied you service because of how you seemed. Or treated you with contempt. My characters moved around the island freely. They had big Christmas limes, went clubbing together, had parties on the beach. They played Carnival together. One year, their band was called 'The Garden of Epicurus' and they dressed like Greeks and Romans with laurels on their heads and roamed the polyglot streets of Port of Spain drinking and dancing and wining and loving one another without fear. I had seen such scenes before. I had been in such bands. It felt true. It was true. I wanted it to be the whole truth.

But one day, I found myself writing a subplot around one of the friends, Fidel. I found myself going in a direction I did not want to go. A path of darkness and doubt and self-loathing and unhappiness. Like me, Fidel was an only child whose mother had died in childbirth. He had trouble accepting who he was, starved himself, fought with his friends, pretended in public that he was straight. Instead of continuing his story, I killed him off in a car crash before he could infect the rest of the writing, like pruning a blighted limb from a plant. Yet, the excision became the conduit for other doubts to spring.

What was I writing? What was the point of writing?

When Dorian left after that first night of lovemaking, I downloaded a picture of him from Facebook and saved it to my phone. I added it to his contact details so that whenever he called or messaged me, I could see him. I could see his dark hair, the pink of his plump but dry lips, the feathery down of his stubble, the pools of his eyes reflecting whatever people wanted to project into them. In this photo, he was wearing black-rimmed glasses that made him look smart, yet also distant.

I couldn't stop thinking about how he tasted, the shock of removing his clothes and seeing him naked for the first time, the way his animal body was an arc of yearning, centred around a surprisingly rough tip – the long, thick, hard digit, pointing at me. It was as though despite everything he had said, every vow he had made, there was this one undeniable thing he could not control. And it was oriented directly at me, couldn't resist me, needed to be near me. It disturbed me to think of it, all this time chaffing against his heavy khaki shorts, all this time hidden throughout all of our innocent romping, through all of our long conversations, the times he had come over just to talk, just to drink beer, just to be friends: this hidden and denied need.

3.

It wasn't long before Granderson got fed up of Dorian.

Granderson had a tattoo parlour on the Avenue. He had a quote from Philip Roth ("Nothing lasts and yet nothing passes either") tattooed on his arm. He had a silver nose ring. And black studs in his ears. He wore lots of black t-shirts. We'd met at a trendy film screening in an abandoned warehouse in Laventille years ago. It was early evening and the warehouse was sweltering. I was sweating from head to toe but my ride wanted to stay and I stayed because I really wanted to see the film (a documentary about Sam Selvon). Granderson was sitting next to me and offered me his bottled water. From that moment, we became friends. Later roommates.

I'm not sure about that guy, Granderson said one morning. I was taken aback because mornings were not his thing, seemed to render him a grunting, non-communicative, chain-smoking, black coffee junkie.

We all have issues, I said, glancing at his Roth tattoo as I tucked into my coconut bake and sausage. And didn't you encourage me to start this?

Since he's been around, you've stopped writing.

I put my bake down. Typical Granderson. Always saying something that I cannot ignore.

And? What's that got to do with anything?

He's just another distraction for you. What are you hiding from, really? Are you really going to keep hiding all your life?

When I fucked Dorian that night, I made sure Granderson could hear the bed banging.

You're on fire tonight, I've never come so fast, Dorian said. He kissed me in a way that felt different, as though the fire that was happening in my gut had rubbed off on him.

4.

I enjoyed having sex with Dorian but he had this way of saying irritating things. Every time we stripped, he'd keep repeating I'm not looking for a relationship, I'm not looking for a relationship, I'm not looking for a relationship, I'm not looking for a relationship, and it would piss me off because I had long come to accept that he wasn't.

At the same time, he seemed to be really into me, would cry whenever he came inside me. Some nights, he'd hold my hands and kiss me deeply, other nights he'd avoid holding my hands, avoid kissing, would choke and slap and spit on me. Sometimes he'd let himself fall asleep and spend the night, other times he'd say he had to make an early start the next day and leave.

Occasionally, he'd invent odd excuses not to come over. Then, he'd come over anyway. At one stage, he said he was learning German online and wouldn't have as much time to hang out. I told him it was good to further his education and encouraged him. But then he started coming over more regularly and I never heard about the course again. Another time he said his license had expired and he couldn't drive anymore so he couldn't come see me. That same night, he came.

At first I thought he was doing the whole player routine of

keeping people on their toes. Then I realised it wasn't premeditated. It was just messy. People were sometimes messy. He was just messy. Really messy.

Dorian was fascinated by gender and drag and fluidity. Yet, he'd say transphobic things. When the body of Anastasia Fierce, a local drag queen, was found in a park a few blocks from where I lived, he said that's what happened when you were a whore who did tricks in Nelson Mandela Park.

How could you say that? I could hear my pitch raise. I looked at him incredulously.

It's true, these people take stupid risks, he continued, his tone casual.

That's victim blaming. I thought you were a feminist?

She wasn't a woman.

Oh my god.

When he noticed I'd bought a candle from the gay couple who had made a name for themselves selling fancy household items, he said those bullers are so lame. When we watched Ru Paul's Drag Race he said Gottmik was crazy because who would want to transition to become a man just to pretend to be a woman.

It's drag, I said, it's about having the freedom to be anywhere on a spectrum. She's saying it's okay to be a man and to be effeminate at the same time. I dig it.

He was in his late twenties and a little younger than me, but not by much. Sometimes I'd win him over and get him to see my point of view. Other times, I'd get sick of it and decide I wouldn't have these types of conversations with him anymore. And then we'd fuck and it was as though everything was recalibrated, everything forgivable. He'd tell me about his past, his childhood living on San Pedro Estate, the day his parents stopped speaking to him because he was queer, and he'd tell me how much he missed the idea of a family, a real family, how hard life sometimes seemed for him, knowing his own flesh and blood had effectively banished him from their lives, and I'd cuddle him and tell him it was okay, he could choose his family now. The writer in me felt this was the key to the riddle of him. I saw him as a character in a novel who went through life always testing people, always provoking everyone around him, always trying to find out whom he could trust because, deep down, he felt his life was out of his control.

We'd go for walks in the Botanical Gardens after the rain. There'd be mist hanging over the Northern Range. President's House would look like it was made of gingerbread and sugar. The flowers would bloom fragrantly, their delicate stamens, their otherworldly shapes, the colours and patterns that seemed prettier than any Carnival fabric, would all sing from a hymn sheet of praise for all things kind and beautiful – all of it was a new place we were discovering, a new path.

Or we would have tea at Mount St Benedict, the monastery at the heart of the island, and we would watch the humming-birds feed. He'd stand still, completely still, and the birds would come sit on his soft, beautiful hands. I never saw anything like it.

Then, one night after sex he said he didn't like kissing. I laughed but when I looked at him he wasn't joking. I told him we could stop. But then he kissed me, as though with gratitude. I felt something in the room move, some object. But when I looked nothing had shifted.

5.

We had been sleeping together for three months when Dorian disappeared. He didn't call or visit. He didn't read my messages. No one in the mas camp on Murray Street had heard from him in over a year when I checked. For someone who once worked as a social media manager, his social media accounts were shockingly neglected. His last update had been years ago. Over breakfast one Sunday, Granderson gave me a look that said I told you so. But instead, he just said, I'm sorry.

I kept telling myself I didn't mind being ghosted. But then I'd be folding my clothes and I would think of him and it would be like I was processing everything that had happened and the act of folding and sorting my shirts and trousers became synonymous with accepting it all.

Around this time, yet another murder happened. Granderson saw the newpaper report on Facebook and showed it to me.

PAGEANT CONTESTANT STABBED TO DEATH AT HOME

INVESTIGATORS are probing what they believe to be a domestic dispute which they say led to the murder of a man on Wednesday.

Officers said they were summoned to the house occupied by Mikey Shah at Emerald Drive, El Dorado, around 6.30pm.

When they arrived at the premises, they found the body of the former pageant contestant in a bedroom. A close male friend of Shah is helping with the investigation.

Police say there were no signs of forced entry and nothing valuable was missing prompting them to believe Shah knew his killer.

I put the phone down. I worried. Where was Dorian? I gave him a call. There was no answer.

The next day my phone rang.

What's up stranger, Dorian said.

I felt foolish for thinking anything had happened to him. I felt foolish for wanting an excuse to call him. And I felt something else, perhaps it was happiness, at the mere sound of his voice.

Glad you're alive, I said and immediately I felt pathetic and regretted it.

Why wouldn't I be?

Don't you read the news?

Oh that guy, yeah saw that. I just can't believe it. Who are these men who let these wackos into their bedroom?

It rose to the surface, that flicker, that spark of hesitation I'd felt before, the little grain of uncertainty that you know will snowball into an objection too big to dismiss but you play along for the moment anyway.

That sounds like you're blaming the victim, I said. How is that any different from saying a woman should be careful who she brings into her bedroom? Aren't you a feminist? As I spoke, the conversation felt like déjà vu.

I was talking to my friends about this all day yesterday, he said. I think if guys want to end up dead in bed wearing a bra and a panty like this guy did then go ahead and invite any old ho into your house. You look for that.

I wanted to say fuck you you're an asshole and hang up. But part of me, that endlessly stupid and compassionate part, wondered if he was simply afraid. I found myself saying: I wish, for your sake, for all of our sakes, that we could live in a world, in a country in which we felt safe, in which our bedrooms were safe spaces. I really do, Dorian.

There was silence on the other line.

You there?

How did you know that's exactly what I needed to hear today?

I'm just old, I said. I know things. I'm afraid too. You're the first person I've trusted in a long while. Normally, I'm para-noid. Call it the writer in me. Call it the self-saboteur.

I know, he said, I've sometimes felt a distance between us. That's why I've been a little quiet lately. But I just hoped maybe you'd break through it and see that I've got your back.

6.

A few nights later it occurred to me. In everything I'd read about the murder, there was no mention of the victim being found wearing a bra and a panty.

Did Dorian make up this detail? Did he imagine it? Was it meant to be a flourish to his rhetorical point? Did he see bras and panties as degrading, mean it as some kind of smear? Was it something people were saying? Did he hear it from his friends?

Or was there some other reason why he would know such a detail?

I scoured my entire relationship with him, I re-examined his contradictions, the way he'd be fine one minute then a little spaced out the next, all of the homophobic things he would say, things that I attributed to a kind of self-hatred common in the community. But could it have been something else? I even reassessed the way he dressed – the casual, seemingly harmless white boy look, the board shorts, the khaki trousers with deep pockets that might easily hold a knife, a knife that might be needed only once after a period of earning a victim's trust. I thought of all of his pretences to see me: the job letters, the times he just turned up outside and we'd go to isolated places. The things he said about LGBTQ people, though he was one. Or at least seemed to be one. How he had said he was done with the gay community.

He would be the perfect serial killer. No one would suspect a cute Trini white boy of being a psychotic gay-basher.

I did not know what was worse: that I could think this about someone I loved or that it could actually be true and I had fallen for him, or that the first thought that came to my head after thinking all this was how it would make a great novel.

I made sure not to call Dorian for a while, to put some distance between us, to give myself room to understand my thoughts.

Was I being paranoid? Was my writer's imagination overtaking me? Or was I simply seeing the truth? The truth that this relationship was not working and I needed a way out? Or the truth that he was possibly a narcissistic maniac? Should I call the police?

I asked around and a lot of people who knew Dorian spoke about how two-faced he was. He'd go to see movies he didn't want to see. He'd speak politely with people. Then, as soon as they turned their backs, he'd bad-talk them. At university, his favourite text was *The Art of War*, and he was obsessed with this text, a fact he had once mentioned in passing to me. And the more I looked, the more I had the sinking feeling that there was no way of knowing who the real Dorian was. He didn't even have an updated social media trail. Which of his many faces was true?

One day he called me and I ignored his call. But then I panicked and called him back.

We talked the way we always did, and I found myself slipping into those warm sea waves again: that sparkling feeling he gave me, the feeling that sustained me for hours and hours as we spoke over the phone. And somehow the conversation moved on to a mutual acquaintance and Dorian started to say how much he disliked this guy and I wondered whether he was saying bad things about the guy now in private but would sweet talk him to his face. Anger welled inside me and I decided to test something.

I bet you must bad-talk me a lot behind my back, I said.

Oh no I tell everyone how wonderful you are.

I said I needed to go because someone was calling and hung up.

7.

He called back to say he wanted to come over later that night. I told him I was busy, maybe we could see each other next week. I knew he had abandonment issues because of what had happened with his family. But there was no way in hell I was letting a potential serial killer into my house again.

8.

After a while, he stopped calling. And it was when he stopped trying to reach out that I wanted him all over again.

9.

One night, when I was home alone, I called Dorian. I told him I could never see him again.

He didn't reply. He hung up the phone.

Later that night, I sat at my desk. Buster came up to me, sniffed me a little as though testing my mood to see if I was okay. Satisfied, he assumed his regular position in the nook by my legs. I had a few hours before dawn.

I knew that what I was about to commit to paper was

something I needed to distance myself from, to put behind me and, in the process, maybe, just maybe, leave space for something real to grow.

I would write a story about Dorian. Maybe the writing would help me figure everything out, sort it all out. Maybe it would take me to something I was yet to discover, the way a relationship takes you to places and moments you never saw coming. Maybe, at last, I would write something true.

And then, I heard the jeep pull up outside. After a while, he dimmed his headlights. There was a knock on my door. Buster barked.

I thought of answering. From the desk, I looked out my window at the old mango tree growing next door, its leaves silver, its limbs gently swaying in the wind. Rain was coming.

I ignored the knocking.

I began to write.

ACKNOWLEDGEMENTS

Versions of some of these stories were published at *adda*, Akashic Books' *Duppy Thursdays*, and *Hemingway Shorts* (Hemingway Foundation of Oak Park, 2020).

Thank you Jeremy Poynting, Jacob Ross, Hannah Bannister, Breanne and Brandon Mc Ivor, Caroline Mackenzie, Sharda Patasar, Sanjay Saith, Arden Heerah, Rajiv Mohabir, Garth Greenwell and the Sunday Afternoon Crew, Arnold Rampersad, Muli Amaye, Opal Palmer Adisa, Alexia Arthurs, Olive Senior, Barbara Jenkins and Chaplin Copernicus Bagoo. For the inspiration of their work, I additionally thank Ifeona Fulani, Pauline Melville, Lawrence Scott ('Preludes' is in dialogue with Scott's 'A Dog is Buried'), Greg Thorpe ('1960' is after Thorpe's '1961'), and Jameson Fitzpatrick (whose poetry yielded the title for 'Selected Boys: 2013-2016'). Finally, I must thank Kate Bush for helping me up this hill.

ABOUT THE AUTHOR

Andre Bagoo is a poet and writer, the author of four previous books, including the poetry collections *BURN* (Shearsman, 2012) and *Pitch Lake* (Peepal Tree Press, 2017) and a book of essays, *The Undiscovered Country* (Peepal Tree Press, 2020), which was winner the non-fiction category of the 2021 OCM Bocas prize for Caribbean Literature. He was awarded The Charlotte & Isidor Paiewonsky Prize in 2017 and shortlisted for the Ernest Hemingway Foundation's annual fiction prize in 2020.

Pitch Lake
ISBN: 9781845233532; pp. 105; pub. 2017; price £8.99

Divided into three sections, Andre Bagoo's poems explore the multiple resonances of the words, where pitch signifies both the stickiness of memory – the way the La Brea Pitch Lake is a place where "buried trees [are] born again" – and the idea of scattering: of places and impressions and the effort to hold them in one vision. The first part brings together poems that encompass reflections on art; Trinidad as a fallen Eden with its history of slavery and the inhumanity of "cachots brulants"; Black Lives Matter; visits to Britain and the image of cows "straight out of Hardy"; and poems about finding love in a climate of homophobia. In the second section, poems with an elaborated discursive structure sit next to little imagist poems written in response to Trinidad's disappearing fauna and threatened eco-system.

The third section, "Lake", is a sequence of prose poems, varying in length, some surreal, suggestive rather than explicit, presenting subtly dislocated narratives that, even in a short space, disrupt the reader's expectations of where they are heading. In their brevity, these prose pieces offer surfaces, like that of a lake, that invite the reader to wonder what lies underneath but warn that this is not necessarily what is most predictable.

In *Pitch Lake*, Andre Bagoo, author of the Bocas prize shortlisted poetry collection, *BURN*, displays a continuing commitment to exploration and experiment.

The Undiscovered Country
ISBN: 9781845234638; pp. 196; pub. 2020; price, £12.99

Winner of the OCM Bocas Non-fiction Prize for Caribbean
Literature.

"A manifesto, a literary criticism, a personal chronicle of
literary life, a book of days, a stage wherein famous writers such
as Walcott, Thomas, Gunn, Espada, and others become actors,
The Undiscovered Country discovers many things, but one thing
for sure: Andre Bagoo is a fearless, brilliant mind. He can take
us from the formal critical perspective to new futurist 'visual
essay', to verse essay, to sweeping historical account that is
unafraid to go as far in time as Columbus and as urgently-of-
our moment as Brexit – all of it with precision and attentive-
ness to detail that is as brilliant as it is startling. Bravo." — Ilya
Kaminsky, author of *Deaf Republic* and *Dancing in Odessa*.

Andre Bagoo asks interesting questions (was there an alterna-
tive to the independence that Trinidad sought and gained in
1962?) and is open to trying out where his ideas take him. His
interest in the world around him encompasses literature, art,
film, food, politics, even Snakes and Ladders – but he is just as
keen to share with the reader some sense of how his point of
view has been constructed. He writes as a gay man who grew
up in a country that still has colonial laws against gay sexuality,
as a man whose ethnic heritage is both African and Indian in a
country whose politics have been stymied by its ethnic divi-
sions. And just what were the effects of repeat-watching a
defective video of *The Sound of Music*, truncated at a crucial
moment? Encyclopaedic knowledge is rarely the point of the
essay, but few readers will leave this collection without feeling
better informed and more curious about their worlds.